apple harbor

— Book One of the Series —

By Mark W. Helms

PUBLISH AMERICA

PublishAmerica
Baltimore

First printing

ISBN: 1-4137-1161-8
PUBLISHED BY PUBLISHAMERICA, LLLP
www.publishamerica.com
Baltimore

Printed in the United States of America

to my daughters:

Natasha, who now plays with angels

and

Jennifer Lynn, I miss you and pray for you
(whether you like it or not!!)

acknowledgments

My thanks to my parents and sister, who believed in this project and my wife, who bugged me for a year to write the stories down that I had growing up.

A special thanks to Kayla and Isaac. You both were a source of encouragement to me when you were simply being yourself.

Kayla, your joy is contagious, and your love of Jesus Christ is pure.

Isaac, I can't wait to see what becomes of your life. You have such spirit!

contents

apple harbor

— chapter 1 —

Midnight Cry

The mare Star, a quarter horse, would give birth anytime, and Mr. Henderson heard WTRS report unusually cold weather for tonight. So he set plenty of wood into the belly of the wood-burning stove, at the far corner of the stables, with several fans to circulate the heat. I had helped on this farm for a couple of years after school, and Saturdays, mostly I took care of the horses. I'd brush and groom them after letting them stretch out in the pasture, and I rode Jake down some back roads. I'd clean the stables with a rake, shovel and wheel barrel, give them fresh hay and feed, and provide them with clear water from one of the old red pumps located in the stable.

I did all this to ride Jake. I loved that horse. I'd take him on some of the country dirt roads where I'd see the apple and maple trees lining the way to the farmhouse. The trees were white washed, to keep away bugs, deer, and also for folks who might come by at night. I'd ride him through fields of white daisies, orange poppies and blue lupines that mingled together so easily. I'd pass the green rolling hills where I'd hear crickets or see fireflies if I happened to be riding at night with the Hendersons. I'd ride over and around meandering brooks bordered with pines and huge oaks where if I stopped just a moment I could hear songs in the breezes. Of course, just across this brook was a fully functioning Gristmill.

If I was especially ambitious I'd ride the back road to the beach, a three-mile trot, where I could see the tug boats riding out Long Island Sound on Mariner's Drive. Half a mile down this spot were boats crowded at the docks, daysailers and larger yachts. But we never ventured that far. Old Salt had his fishing boat out there, where he'd go out into the North Atlantic for months on end.

Jake loved to ride the incoming waves on the beach. More often than I care to admit I fell off Jake in a thunder of hoof beats and water. I'd spend the afternoons picking up driftwood, exploring the secluded beach with its single lighthouse, Darboughry Point. It was secluded because of the rocks to the east side. But the beach itself was great for wading and Jake and I got our share of that. The residents pretty much kept to the beaches starting about two miles east and west of here. It's probably the quietist beach in all of Connecticut.

You haven't lived till you roasted lobster freshly caught right on the beach.

I did that with Old Salt and my sister once. She hates lobster though. He knows how to cook the lobster right in seawater, and cover it with locally grown corn. There's a trick to doing it right.

Jake was a quarter horse. His sole purpose on the farm was for the pleasure of riding him. The mare, Star, was used for the days the tractor went out along with the other stallion, a Clydesdale named Abe. The only time they were hitched together was when I was thirteen, and I didn't know any better. Mr. Henderson had a good laugh over that, seeing how much I was trying to get Star to keep up. Then Abe would quit and the plowing went into circles. Mr. Henderson quickly unhitched Star and told me, "Abe can handle this alone son." He was very patient with me that day two years before.

My sister Kasie, who at thirteen was two years younger than me, and her friend Christine would feed the animals on Saturday mornings. Kasie had long hair; both of us were medium wavy blonde-headed kids with hazel colored eyes; she was a little thinner than me. She was very hyper, could talk incessantly and seemed to do crazy stuff now and then just because.

Christine has the wildest thick long curly auburn hair with flecks of copper and honey highlights. It was as if her hair betrayed her inner fire, for she was so very quiet otherwise. She had piercing blue eyes and would smile easily, but forget talking.

Until she was three or four years old, her parents never heard a word from her. For that reason alone they assumed she was slow, and were going to take her to a specialist, but my mom mentioned to Christine's mom, Emma Solanski, "She talks to her toys in the backyard all the time." When her parents spied on her they found it to be true. So they started her on music and ballet lessons, which slightly loosened her tongue. To us anyhow. The kids at school hardly ever heard her voice. She did everything to avoid drawing attention to herself, but it happened anyhow. Like when she'd spontaneously dance because she was happy, or the way she'd clasped her hands in joy.

Christine looked younger than Kasie only because Kasie developed faster. At fourteen Christine was somewhat pretty, yet a rather thin girl. She had braces and mild acne (but who didn't have acne?). She was a grade ahead of her peers, in my homeroom class. We shared over half of the same classes growing up, and it was no different this year.

I was sort of heavy but not to where I got picked on over it. Well, not too much. I had lost some weight this year, but kids still call me "Colossal Cooper". Oh well.

The Hendersons had dairy cattle, goats, sheep, chickens, some pigs, ducks, geese, a hound dog, a chow-shepherd and one sheep dog and more cats than I could count.

The cats were supposed to keep the mice population down. The barn had a few owls and half a dozen nests of swallows. To draw water for the animals, Kasie would pump the stubborn hand pump of the kitchen's red pump. Yes, there was a well just outside the farmhouse, but that was for household uses.

"Don't forget to prime the pump child," we'd hear nearly every week. In order to draw the water out we had to pour a little water in, which was drawn from the well. The water from the well wasn't fit for drinking, and the water from the rain barrel was for washing clothes. Working on this farm was like stepping into another era.

We all loved animals so to us this wasn't work at all. It was sheer pleasure!

We were here this day, a Sunday in hopes of seeing one of the mares give birth to her colts. But it didn't happen that morning.

My friend James would help just because he had nothing better to do. He was tall, lanky and sloppy looking with brown hair that looked moppy and touched his large framed glasses. He had a Cheshire cat grin that came after his jokes especially. He liked the 1928 Ford Phaeton that Mr. Henderson was restoring. It was a beautiful yellow car with white wall tires. It was kept in a storage garage, along with his tractors, tools and a biplane. The biplane, which Mr. Henderson used for crop dusting, had canary yellow wings with a navy blue body, and an American Star on each wing.

I asked Mr. Henderson why he had the Stars painted on the wing tops, to which he replied, "If you've ever paid attention to your model planes, your World War Two planes had the Star on the wings, remember? The Stearman was used to train pilots in the early days of the war."

Mr. Henderson looked much younger than his fifty plus years. His manner was quiet, he was easy going and pleasant, tall and thin like James with thick white hair that had to be constantly brushed back from his forehead. He was easy to like.

"Mr. Henderson, you probably have some great stories from the war?" James asked.

"I think I just heard Mom ring the dinner bell son, why don't you two get washed up?"

We didn't have to be asked twice.

Mrs. Henderson made the best breakfast; the eggs, the sausage, pancakes and juice were all fresh. Ever have milk straight from a cow?

"After breakfast you children will need to change quickly into your church clothes, as your parents will meet us there okay? Christina, I'll drive you to your own church, OK hon?" Mrs. Henderson at only five-foot tall was almost as tall sleeping as standing up. She had short curly hair that was permed and colored every other week downtown. She could be excitable at times.

"We'll be back tonight to see Star give birth to a new colt!" Kasie said.

"That's assuming a lot Kasie," James answered her.

"It'll be tonight, I just know it," Kasie said very sure of herself.

Mr. Henderson spoke up. "You know kids, if you'd like, and you can pick a pattern to paint the stables. Maybe you can paint a candy bar wrapper, a cartoon character or perhaps a scene from nature. We can talk about it and I'll decide. What do you think Eldon?"

" I'd love to help on that," I said.

(Everyone who knew me knew I loved art.)

"Maybe James or you girls would have some suggestions?"

"I like the Miami Dolphins," James said

Mrs. Henderson shook her head doubtfully at that, exclaimed, "Well shut my mouth James!! As if we'd paint that on our stables or barn."

Mr. Henderson was going to agree with James I think, but he changed his mind. He had that look like he was going to say something. I knew he liked the Dolphins too.

Christine spoke out. " How about a scene of some doe looking over your fields at sunset with her young?"

"Yes, that sounds promising Christine," Mr. Henderson answered looking at his wife with an expression of his mind being made up.

"Maybe you could put Yellow Bear in that picture?" Christine added.

Mrs. Henderson laughed, answering, "Well Christie, that would make that chow-shepherd put on airs. Yellow Bear already beeps the horn if she thinks I'm taking too long at May's shopping. Did you know she uses her paws to beep the horn? Good gracious grief!"

(Whenever Mrs. Henderson got excited her southern came back.)

"Yellow Bear understands what I'm saying Aunt Betty. I scolded her for tearing those sheets the first time you got her, and she was only a pup but never did it again."

"No, but she likes to knock over garbage if I don't give her a ride every single time I leave the farm, bless her heart, if they put her brain on the head of a pin, it'd roll around like a BB on a six-lane highway."

Christine laughed in spite of herself, saying, "True, but she also tells you when the phone is ringing if you or Uncle Frank are riding the mower or making noise with something. She is a great secretary!"

"How is Craig doing these days honey? I don't see much of him."

"He's very busy with track. I pretty much am lucky to see him between classes myself anymore. I see these friends here a lot more, and he is NOT my boyfriend whatever you might think."

Mrs. Henderson smiled as if she knew better. But Christine didn't like anybody that way at all. Craig talked to her about his problems, and in doing so found himself hanging around the farm sometimes to help. I guess he figured Christine was too quiet to blab his secrets.

The grandfather clock struck eight o'clock, to which Mrs. Henderson said, "Well children, y'all need to get dressed into your church clothes now."

Later that afternoon we saw Star give birth to a colt, which Christine named Midnight Cry. It was the most awesome thing I had ever seen.

"A lot better than seeing a chick hatch; they're soooo ugly." James laughed his toothy laugh.

"You'd look ugly too if you were crammed in that hot sweaty egg James," Kasie said.

We all laughed, partly in the wonder of the moment. Star looked him over and after his initial awkward first steps, Midnight Cry got to his feet (as Mr. Henderson called it) and fed on his mother.

"Isn't he altogether lovely?!" Christine exclaimed. "God, you sure know what you're doing!" She added looking up at the stable ceiling towards heaven. Who could argue with that? Who would? He really was a beautiful new horse, all wet and wonderful.

After a great meal of Creole jambalaya, maple pecan corn bread, black bean soup, sweet and sour pork chops and the finest apple pie, we were driven home.

Christine and Kasie would stay overnight upstairs, at Gram's apartment. My grandmother had lived there for years, since Mom was a teenager. The girls went upstairs immediately. I sat on my makeshift bed downstairs, the couch in our own apartment. The hours passed quickly as I was drawing people.

I remember hearing their chatter upstairs as Gram rocked in her rocker, I could tell she was crocheting by the rhythm of her rocking. I knew Kit Kat, her tabby, loved to lie on her lap making her crocheting difficult, but not impossible.

BOOM BOOM BOOM BOOM!

That was my Uncle Buddy upstairs.

There were times he walked so hard the ceiling tiles had shaken loose in my room. Now I was sleeping on the couch in the living room because last Saturday afternoon Mom wanted the furniture moved around. Mom was concerned about the dust from those tiles being a health hazard, so wanted to move it so it'd be "away from being under the ceiling", however you do that; but all of a sudden when Dad and I had worked on that then she decided other things needed moving around. Everything had been put on top of my bed "for the time being," Dad had said.

So I would sleep on the couch for now.

BOOM BOOM BOOM

"HAVE YOU SEEN THAT CAT? HAVE YOU? HAVE YOU SEEN THAT CAT?!"

"No dear, I haven't," I heard my grandmother lie. She must've had Kit Kat covered up under the blanket she was crocheting, along with that patchwork quilt Gram often wrapped herself up in. Her rocking was slower.

The gas furnace lit my living room up as the line went *Whoosh.*

I always liked that gas furnace and it's blue pilot light. The flames had a way of making me feel very peaceful. The blue light bulb I screwed in from my bedroom helped too.

Once, when I was about eight, my uncle Jim had told me that God keeps the heavens blue so the angels could see better while singing. He had a blue light bulb in the guest room, which was used as a nightlight. So I've had a blue light bulb ever since.

— chapter 2 —

Troubles

When I got up I skipped breakfast, as I had to get Christine's help. I had hurried through my shower but Dad went into the bathroom and said, " Eldon, this soap is as dry as a bone." So I had to shower again. Then Mom complained merely because I hadn't dried my hair or body before I got dressed. I had my paper route and the dogs and then... Kasie just gave me a look as she came in the door and complained loudly. "Gross! You ever hear of a comb and brush? You are needed upstairs."

So, I went upstairs with Kasie, comb and brush in my right hand, towel wrapped around my head, and hearing Mom complain about my drenched clothes. So they had a clingy look to them, I had things to do. " You look like a mummy," Christine giggled at the sight of this strangely wrapped creature dripping in the kitchen.

"I got to dry my hair a sec. Only be a sec," I said, headed for the bathroom and was out in two shakes. I threw the towel on the floor and was done wasting time.

My grandmother had things arranged in her apartment in a very cozy way. Comfort was just a part of her home, every item brought peace and rest to the cold weary heart. My grandmother knew that putting vines in the windows set a mood, her many afghans and crocheted comforters strewn over the couch and sofa chairs and rocker also loaded with pillows.

Oh, and she had snacks. THIS FIFTEEN-YEAR-OLD LOVED TO EAT. Between her books, of which she had so many, were various boxes of crackers and tins of cookies. Butter cookies. It was always butter cookies near some Dickens book.

Christine smiled looking around at everything. That was something you'd never miss about Christine, her smile. She had about five of them when most people only have one and seem reluctant to use it.

Gram sat there, so engrossed in her reading, that I'd thought she didn't notice us. What was she reading? It was a Borky the detective dog comic book I had drawn up, issue number 1 where Borky moved to Venice on the first floor.

"I can see the gondolas floating overhead from here," Gram was reading out loud. "And I know I'll better be able to catch that fiendish pizza thief, somewhere lurking in Venice, the city that never sleeps! With my scuba gear and scuba pizza box, I'll be sure to capture that fiend!"

Gram was laughing. Fortunately, it was meant to be funny. The thief turns out to be a cat with a Robin Hood complex, our own Kit Kat, who had delivered a bunch of pizzas to a gifted musician boy who didn't know he was gifted, but somehow Kit Kat knew, and by the delivering of these wonderful pizzas he was sooo inspired that when he found a broken violin in the dumpster behind orchestra hall, which only had two strings left, he picks it up, plays it, and is immediately recognized as a super musician. So, of course all of the pizza places drop the charges if Kit Kat agrees to be their mascot, and the boy play for them. Borky thinks this is a wonderful solution, case closed!

Christine said, "I wish it was that easy to play my violin and make a difference in the world."

"Oh, you're wonderful Christine! I love how you play!" my gram said.

"Thanks Mrs. Lewis. Nice window. Water lilies in stain glass! Why I didn't notice that last night but with the sunlight peeking through I see it's altogether lovely!" Christine exclaimed.

"My cousin Joe broke the other one playing baseball, so Dad got this one from the Anson Baptist Church before they demolished the old building," I explained.

"He must've been playing in the street then from here there's no yard nearby."

"Exactly. We played between traffic Christine."

Some Jimmy Durante piano music was playing on the radio, it was pretty funny hearing that raspy voice. I could have lingered here a bit longer if maybe school was off, and I didn't have the paper route. I knew she had hot cocoa on the stove for us, made from scratch with real chocolate bars melted into milk, not that cheap powder stuff. I knew she had a crate full of more of our Borky the detective dog comic books that James and I made, along with half a dozen boxes of newspaper comics.

"You staying honey?" Gram asked. I think she meant me but she was looking at Christine.

"Wish I could. Just popped into say hey and all, to check on Kit Kat and get Christine. I need to show her my paper route. Got anything to eat Gram?"

(My uncle was pretty dumb about cats and people and anything he had to talk to. So Kasie and I would check on Kit Kat ever so often.)

"Remember I love you but Jesus loves you far more than anyone," Gram said with her brightest smile, pointing to some cookies on the shelf.

"Wow! Butter-oatmeal, I hadn't had those in a while, the kind with raisins too! Thanks Gram!" I grabbed the whole bag for my journey.

"You remember what I said now honey," Gram says.

"You got it."

She always said that stuff about Jesus. It's as if she'd fear when you'd leave you'd be hit by a passing semi and knocked into becoming some crazed senseless heathen. She probably thought as we'd lie dying we'd forget our faith, so she reminded each and every one of us cousins upon leaving that, "Jesus loves you a whole bunch." I bet she even reminded Kit Kat.

"She sure loves you," Christine said after we got down the stairs.

"Aw, she could love the devil himself I think."

"Like I said," Christine added, teasing me.

We had dogs to take care of and papers too. The only way I could do that was to roller-skate the parameter of the town around the valley twice, one run to pick up the dogs on their leashes as I dropped off the papers, the other run to drop off the dogs. Then I'd stop at the pine grove that overlooked the valley. I always stopped there to catch my breath, sort of a sanity break.

On this particular Monday morning Christine came up with me to see what my route was like. She was going to take it over for a few days so I could go on a trip to Washington, DC. that the newspaper sponsored for its carriers. Her *friend* Craig was also going on that trip.

"Dad called last night Eldon. Mr. Henderson's stable burned to the ground."

"WHAT?! Really? Are the horses okay? How about Midnight Cry? Star?"

"Their horses are okay. Dad said Mr. Henderson had to cover their eyes with a blanket in order to lead them out of there."

"He got all three of them horses out then? Well, four including Midnight Cry."

"Yes, all of them including Midnight Cry."

"Did that wood burning stove start the barn fire?" I asked her.

"No, it was on the east side of the barn. The fire marshal thinks it was lightning. The horses are all with the neighboring farms for now."

"I'm going to miss riding that Jake, and the other farms aren't the same."

Christine sadly replied, " I know."

It bothered us both to go on talking about it, so I just started explaining the route.

"Mrs. Markle doesn't like you to come through her front door to pick up Rowzers, just use the garage's side door where she keeps him. See, he already has the leash."

"Where do I put the paper?"

"Spread out right inside the kennel, under the water and food dishes. After you return Rowzers make sure he goes in there."

"But doesn't Mrs. Markle read her paper, I mean—she really wants it spread out inside a kennel?"

"Nope, she hates the *Apple Harbor Journal-Courier*, she never reads it."

"Why?"

"The editor once wrote something unkind about her cooking and she hasn't cared for it since." I looked at Christine who was smirking and quickly added, "The paper I mean, not her cooking."

"When did this happen Eldon?"

"In 1950 I think."

"This guy, is he the same editor today?"

"Oh good grief no! He died before you or I were born."

Christine was completely shocked. Her eyes were wide and gaping as she tried to figure this mystery out.

"That be like me keeping my violin on the shelf as a knick-knack; subscribing to a newspaper just to use it in a dog's cage!" Christine shook her head in total disbelief. Adults amazed us sometimes.

I chatted a lot with Christine these days. At the farm she seemed to open up, so our friendship did too. She was the quietest girl at school, and I took second place. But I could talk to her when I couldn't talk to anyone else too much. Well, you know about James my other friend. But with Christine I could say whatever I had on my mind without it being analyzed to death.

"Poverty stinks," I said, as we walked on.

"What do you mean?"

"Okay, look at all these houses with their paint peeled off, they look trashy."

"Mmmmmm, smell that sea salt Eldon? That is what makes the paint peel."

"Look at how my grandmother had to save for everything all her life. Her bum of a son is living with her and all he does is drink."

"She's happy. Not because she's being abused but, well, why do you suppose that is?"

The dogs got into a bit of a fight as we passed this brown orange spotted cat, and that broke up my train of thought. Christine laughed very hard and said, "Maybe I'll get your sister Kasie and James to help me with the dogs." We went to drop off the last dog, a collie named Lass along with the master's newspaper.

Looking over the valley as the peach sunrise broke up the violet haze of night, Christine was in awe of the beauty of it all. She had that look on her face as she gazed around, as if she were drinking everything in... and was satisfied completely with nature's results. I had to say something; everything was having a go at me!

"Hear that? My train, old Number 7 is blowing her whistle!" I said. "Competing with all these early song birds, yeah!!" I had to laugh; I loved that sound!

Christine smiled in acknowledgment.

As a small child I used to groan hearing those train whistles but as years went on they were more a lullaby than a noise. Number 7 was the oldest train on the line, dating back to the 1880's. Her whistle had a sharp piercing ring to it, which was balanced by the low rumbles of the coal engine's thunder. I just loved trains, but especially that one. I momentarily forgot the bad news Christine shared with me.

Christine said, "I'm hearing angel wings whisper to me in this very pine grove," as the breezes lifted the branches. Christine was always seeing angels in every cloud formation, or something wonderful behind the most normal, boring, dull things. She was not weird, but only gifted with a different way of seeing life.

I caught myself sniffing the scents she mentioned sniffing here. She had said it with such exuberance. "OH, the pine, smell the sea salt, and the lilies, oh, and even the lavender, it's all mingled together after such refreshing rain so it's become... God's cologne!"

"Lilies don't make for cologne," I had said, rolling my eyes.

"Well, they do with sea salt and rain, it's manly then."

I couldn't argue with that. It might be true after all.

"This is my sanity break stop, to breathe, to think, to be still, after getting beat up by these evil poodles," I said.

"Evil poodles? Whatever Eldon!"

I had wanted to show her this place knowing how she feels about nature and to cheer us up over that bad news. At that moment we were just going to drop off "Lass" at Mrs. Rowe's house, my last dog after my stop here. It was hard to skate with miniature poodles, chows and Dalmatians leashed together, but after a few years of my paper route, and dog route, I had gotten the hang of it. But my ankles needed the rest after a hard run with those crazy dogs, so I welcomed this stop.

"I guess the breezes do sound like angel wings," I said to Christine.

As stars were flickering out like fireflies taking a nap, I caught the sound of several church bells echoing simultaneously. It was very reassuring to know that time was still rolling in such an orderly way.

"Earlier this spring the old bell crashed down the belfry of the Sunny Valley Baptist Church, Christine. Pastor John got Mike Kuncick to jerry-rig together speakers and sound-system so that for two weeks now in the morning the bell would seem to chime. If the bell didn't chime the Wallstien's cows wouldn't milk properly as they just were used to a certain routine. They had to fool the cows. But they kept this plan a secret from everyone, only Mike told me. Now I'm telling you but don't spread it around! The Wallstiens sang in the choir and paid for three of the church additions, so of course Pastor John didn't want to offend their cows."

"Offend cows?" She laughed. "You guys can't even keep a secret to not offending cows?!"

"I figured I knew what Pastor John needed Mike for. He sure was secretive about the whole thing when he called Mike over that day to his booth."

"What booth?"

"At Tinti's restaurant."

"Naturally." Christine smirked, brushing a wave of amber hair away from her face with her hand.

"ANYWAYS I heard them whispering about a bell. At the time I couldn't figure why he was hiring him to help haul a bell…"

"Mike Kuncick is too skinny to haul a bell Eldon."

"Exactly my thoughts… He wanted him to jerry-rig a recording of a bell, which in another week or so they'll have replaced with a bell from an old train. Unless the church votes otherwise."

"I think people will know it's not a real bell. They're not stupid."

" Did you know? When you heard it this week?" I asked her.

" Well, I guess not Eldon, but still, come on!"

"Mike's fries almost got cold but I rescued them. I also rescued his bacon cheeseburger. Mike didn't even notice his food had been rescued, he just ran out of Tinti's. So I was stuck paying the bill. Can you believe that Christine?"

"You rescued it? Is that what they call it now Eldon?"

"It was awfully good Christine, it could've died an ignominious death in a garbage disposal."

Mrs. Henderson drove by in her husband's pick up just as we were talking.

"Boy, come here, I need your help, you too Christie sugah."

We didn't ask questions; we got in the pick up.

"Pastor John gave us permission to leave the chicks with the church for a week until we can find them homes."

"Homes? For chicks? Why not just butch…"

(Christine interrupts elbowing me!).

"Aunt Betty, when will you be rebuilding your barn then?"

"We're not sure we can Christie. We missed one payment of the insurance, just last week our policy lapsed so of course the fire happened. It's crazy; I simply forgot to mail the payment in. The fire destroyed the stables and spread to the coops. It might be more than we can afford just now honey."

"What will you do then?"

"Probably have to sell the farm Eldon."

"That's not fair! Your husband had this farm in the family for generations." (I was pretty ticked to say the least!).

"Since the war for independence," Mrs. Henderson answered with a heavy sigh.

"The tree house and that tire swing, the air strip where Mr. Henderson zooms off, the split fence and… everything, gone? This year!" I exclaimed.

Christine asked fearfully, "Crackers the white call duck, Yellow

Bear, Star, Midnight Cry, the baby geese, your pigs, goats…all of them?"

Christine looked ready to cry.

"Just pray for a miracle children, pray hard for a miracle."

"It's NOT FAIR! I've invested too many memories here!"

Christine exclaimed, completely exasperated.

In the back of the pick up were five crates of baby chicks all squawking terribly. I think they shared Christine's mood. Mrs. Henderson's and mine too frankly.

Mrs. Henderson kept doing the stick a terrible disservice, grinding the gears till they cried. Christine was all squished up front having to move her legs first left, and then right, so Mrs. Henderson could shift. If that was shifting. It felt more like leaping the gears. Which didn't do much to help the chicks' disposition in the back.

"That fire, Aunt Betty, Daddy told me how upset you were. I didn't know it could cost you everything!" Christine sighed.

"Your daddy is a fine officer Christy," she said trying to smile, but then grumbled about Helen Shmidt and some other folks who wouldn't take her chicks in.

"Now boy, you go look out to see if anyone is near the church and MAKE SURE AS CERTAIN NO ONE IS NEARBY, YOU HEAR ME?" She parked in an alley away from the church and grumbled some more about her cruel inconsiderate neighbors.

"I thought you said you had permission Mrs. Henderson? I don't like this sneaking around," I explained.

"Yeah, from Pastor John, not the whole of Connecticut!"

I hid behind a trashcan watching carefully, no one was around anywhere near the church. We quickly put the crates in the warmest room of the whole church, the library. Christine was talking to Mrs. Henderson as we unloaded the chicks.

"Listen, don't be too quick to sell your farm, I believe something will work out."

"It's not just the barn darling it's a lot of things."

"You want to sell then?"

"Absolutely not. I love that farm. Dad loves the farm."

"Dad?" I interrupted.

"My husband. We have six adult children remember? It sticks."

"Oh, yeah, he calls you Mom too."

"Cover them with these blankets honey... Christy?" Mrs. Henderson was pointing to the crates to her from the pickup window.

"Oh, okay, they're kind of thin though."

Christine placed them on very carefully, allowing for air. She locked them down with clothespins.

"This will have to do until old Smokey Franks fixes the coops up," Mrs. Henderson said.

"Where will the coops go?" Christine asked.

"Believe it or not, in the church's shed. It'll be a temporary fix."

As they were talking I accidentally closed the library door, which locked it.

"Oops!" I announced, very embarrassed.

"Eldon, could you go to the office and see if you can find a key?"

"Sure Mrs. Henderson."

As I was heading towards the church office, I heard the bells go off in the tower. It was late for that I thought. But the bells sounded funny, real slow like the battery in the recorder was dying. So I'm sure certain cows were offended.

That noise echoed throughout the church, then I could hear the sounds of hundreds of scared baby chicks going crazy. The sound of an old distorted church bell playing in their ears from Mike's tape recorder that was not getting enough power... to the chicks it must've sounded very foreboding!

"ELDON!! HURRY UP! SOME FOOL MUST'VE PUT THE SOUND EQUIPMENT IN THE LIBRARY!! OH, LORD, HELP US ALL!! WE'RE IN BEEEGG TROUBLE!!"

"These keys don't work Mrs. Henderson." I said it too calmly, which didn't help the situation any. I wasn't upset enough for Mrs. Henderson. She gave me a look like I was crazy and heartless.

In less than ten minutes we saw the bright red and blue lights of the police cars surrounding the Baptist church and Pastor John looking pretty distraught. We didn't even hear Pastor John knocking on the door as we were trying so hard to get to the chicks. Mrs. Henderson could yell over a SWAT team, if you know what I mean, and with the "CHEAP CHEA CHE CHEP CHIP" sounds going through the church, we couldn't hear ourselves think even.

Pastor John could not get into the church. He was telling Officer Frank Solanski that he had loaned his church keys to Mrs. Henderson late last night. Usually the side door was left open anyways, but we had locked it so as not to be bothered.

"Don't you keep a spare set of keys in your office?"

Officer Solanski was asking Pastor John just outside the door.

"I loaned them to Mrs. Henderson. I can't get in the office without my keys so I can't get in the door to get to the office, and… ah Frank, what do we do?"

I didn't want to go out there. No wayyyy! But I didn't want to be here either, with Mrs. Henderson looking just as distraught.

"Christine, your dad's outside," I said, trying to solve my problem.

Like I said, they kind of looked upset. With all the CHEAP CHEAPING going on, Pastor John was pacing in circles and he looked like one of those Saturday afternoon movie victim wannabes of the bug creature who eats Tokyo… buildings and all.

"Well, I do keep five sets in the church office, but I… uh, can't get in there now without a…" Pastor John said meekly.

"Maybe you could ask your deacons?"

"Daddy! " Christine was pulling on his sleeve. "The side door is now open."

I went to Tinti's, deciding I didn't have time for this craziness. However, after everything got settled down, Christine decided to talk to Pastor John in his office while her dad waited in the next room for her.

"Pastor John, I'd like you to consider asking your church to sponsor a fundraiser."

"For?"

"The Hendersons to build a new barn," Christine answered.

"That'll be more than cookie sales you know."

"Well, I don't have all the details worked out but..."

"How about if you ask them?"

Her voice got very quiet as she said...

"Me? I'm only fourteen years old. I... I ca... can't ask the church."

" Why not?"

"I can't get in front of a million people and ask them for permission."

"We have only two hundred people in our church."

"Might as well be a million." (She turned quite pale just thinking about it.)

"You are in drama at school, right?"

"Yeah, but I play non speaking parts, like an extra."

"Well, I understood you take speech or debate classes."

"Only a few students debate sir. I just listen. Very quietly."

"I can have something printed up in the newsletter, but I think perhaps you should consider asking the church yourself too."

"I'll... I... ppuh... pray about it, okay?"

"That's good enough for me; in the meantime I'll give you a list of folks who need help getting rid of their junk. For now just get some of your friends together to gather it in boxes in their garages. Either we'll sell it in some kind of fundraiser or trash it all."

"How'd you know I'd ask?"

"I didn't Christine. These people have big attics. They've asked me to find young people to help them get rid of stuff for over a year. Your request is very, let's say, providential. We can get Eldon to help. This afternoon. Maybe his sister too."

"He might have other plans."

"Not after this morning he won't."

Christine left his office looking very queasy.

— chapter 3 —

Tinti's

Like I said, I went to Tinti's. In those days Tinti's was a marriage between a restaurant and coffee/ ice cream shop. Babbs had been a waitress there since the foundation was being laid in 1942, bringing hot coffee to the construction boys from her home.

She was our local legend, never wrote her orders and never ever messed up. I liked it simply because for a half hour I could read a comic book in the corner, away from the bells and chimes above the entrance which would first announce me, then five minutes later, in this exact order: Judge Parker, the mayor, the Hanson twins, Russ Peters and Bobby O'Brien, Craig Roman who was Christine's albatross… or guy friend, and then Fred and his shadow Jenkins, fiftyish, old guys who worked the Town Green. They were among the young men who built this place so many years ago. Then they went to war. They had been friends over thirty years, Fred and Jenkins. Almost expected an 'Inc.' at the end of their names, we heard it said together so much. They always ordered: coffee/black and four eggs scrambled with cheese/ small 8 oz. steak one rare/one burnt / fried taters and juice.

Scattered between the pictures on the wall were small eucalyptus trees, ivy vines, and aloe vera plants, Victorian couches and sofa chairs. It looked like a living room in a jungle almost. Except for the counter and tables with there checkered top tablecloths, and carved cafe chairs with the claws holding the ball at the base.

In this jungle you had a bookcase filled with books, mostly classic and several milk jugs cleaned and cut out for the Sunday comics, and a fireplace. In the middle of the next room, the banquet room, was a potbellied stove which still worked, and hundreds of various sized and colored steel pipes going in so many crisscrossed directions, coming out of the ceiling. I imagine the plumber who ever worked on them needed a road map. The orange ones were for steam heat pipes leading to the radiators found at every corner of every room. They never worked too well. Made lots of banging, but after 8 AM no one could tell because of all the regular customers who showed up. So of course bossman used the fireplace and potbellied stove a lot in winter. Whatever works. Oh, Bossman was a middle aged Italian man who owned the place.

Thursday mornings the Yankee Quitter's Club met here, in the banquet room. Helen Smhidt was their chairwoman, and she just walked in. She was a small heavyset lady with a black Brillo-pad hairstyle. The corners of her mouth drooped down permanently and she walked hunkered down as if carrying the weight of Apple Harbor on her back.

"How's your little girlfriend, your partner in crime?" She managed a weak smile. I had given up telling her Christine, who at fourteen was a whole year younger than me, was not my girlfriend and responded as always. "She's fine. James is good too." Then I remembered to add, "Thanks for asking."

I wanted to be polite after all. It was the least I could do.

She walked over to the men at the counter. "I'm sure you heard about the church bell over at that Baptist Church?" she crowed.

"I thought you called it that stinking Baptist Church Helen?" Jenkins wouldn't swear for my benefit. He refused to look her way however.

"Those weren't her exact words," Fred laughed. "Say Helen, I bet you picked that up on your police scanner at home, never has it off Eldon," Fred growled a bit, imitating her, looking at me. "Never has it off!" Fred's smile revealed he was just playing, he reminded me a lot of a pastor or kind teacher, with his conservative haircut and cheerful disposition. He seemed to blend in to any situation well, his clothes although a workman's seemed to appear fancier among the wealthier friends he had, yet the same outfit would appear threadworn and tattered among the poorer customers. He didn't change his clothes or his manners. It was just Fred's attitude of acceptance; still, Helen seemed to bring out of Fred a gentle scolding. Now Helen gave me a look.

I didn't say anything, just shrugged my shoulders. Helen looked to me for some sort of reassurance, but all I could do was smile rather sheepishly.

"Well, we're taking up a collection for it, that's all. It's my first order of business."

"Well, that's nice Helen, really," Fred said, trying to be understanding.

"I thought your hens had other business Helen," Jenkins said. He didn't have a soft side. His face reflected the look of a man used to frowning, to venting his anger, his very hair appeared bristly and hard, crew cut marine-style haircut complete with white wall sides. Everything about him was tight and thin, yet he was well muscled for his age and unapproachable. His eyes narrowed when he saw me watching their conversation. I looked away from him; I wasn't intimidated but was wary of Mr. Jenkins. I was pretending to read my comic but of course I couldn't. I knew something hung in the air between them; it had to be a bitter dark horrible thing. Like a gnarly root which overtakes a beautiful garden, sucking the life out of every flower and spreading to the ponds and killing everything in its sight. They wouldn't talk about it in front of me.

Helen left for the banquet room.

A shaft of sunlight broke through the clouds as Babbs handed the men their breakfast in her singsong voice.

"Good morning, good morning Mr. Ralph Jenkins and Mr. Fred Murphy!"

"Yes, and a good day to you too Babbs," they said in unison.

The sunlight filled the whole of Tinti's, spreading throughout every corner and flooded everything with brightness and joy. Shadows hid. Babbs was here! Her face had formed into a permanent grin after so many years of laughing; her brown large eyes were accentuated by waves and waves of naturally curly snow-white hair, which she kept very short. She was almost sixty years old, judging by her time at Tinti's. But it didn't show in her face. She looked about forty-five. Her clothes, her mannerisms, everything said she was younger in spite of her white hair.

"Done with your route Eldon?" Babbs asked me.

"Yes."

Without a word she placed a big order of scrambled eggs with cheese, tator tots and a small (?) eight-oz. steak in front of me. Every now and then she'd pay for the meals of some poor stray cat that wandered in. Today I was that cat. I long ago gave up trying to leave a tip big enough to pay for it, because she'd chase me down the street to return it.

Butch Gambill just walked in and sat by the jukebox, out of earshot.

"That the mechanic who worked on your dad's truck, right Eldon? He's more like an artist than a mechanic, that '55 Chevy Bel-Air had been on the blocks for over a year now."

"Yeah, I know, sir, " I said to Mr. Jenkins. "It was only supposed to get a paint job but before we knew it everything was getting refurbished or restored."

Fred looked up from his coffee, brushing light brown hair back from his forehead. His deep blue eyes seemed to smile as he spoke.

"That's his passion, he doesn't charge the few other guys whose vehicles he took to restoring. But guys like Jenkins wanted their trucks back yesterday; he won't bother simply getting it towed to another shop."

Fred laughed. "Still he sure did a good job on old Henderson's Ford."

"Heard he had heart trouble," I said, trying in vain to smooth Jenkins up. Ever try to stop the ocean? Jenkins black eyes blazed with anger as his foolishness gushed forth, like a mighty wave.

"Well, he should've hired a mechanic to fill in. I wonder if I'll ever see my '67 Chevy again? More often than not I go over there to see the 'CLOSED/GO AWAY' sign up. I guess kite flying is more important than fixing my stinking truck; why, he's keeping it hostage, and I might just call Officer Solanski on this one."

Russ Peters and Bobby O'Brien were laughing from across the counter.

Russ said, "Like Frank is at your beck and call ! Give it a rest! Jenkins is only ticked off because Mrs. Markle chewed on him about that chest of drawers he snuck into her garage last weekend. He got busted! His eyes got so big when Mrs. Markle asked him 'What you doing in my garage?'"

"Awww, shut up about that already, don't a man got a right to any privacy Russ?" Jenkins yelled.

"Not when you're being so ignorant." Fred sighed. "That wasn't too bright Jenkins."

"What chest?" I had to ask. Jenkins glared at me before he answered.

"I paid Butch's boy to make me a chest and it was pathetic, the boy's as pitiful as his father."

Fred rebuked his friend. "That was four years ago Ralph; don't be so mean and ornery! The boy won several blue ribbons for his cabinet making at the state fair last summer, so my guess is he's improved. You must've liked the chest as you kept it four years."

Jenkins voice softened up as he answered. "You're right there. I did keep it for four years; it was good for storing tools I guess and junk." Then Jenkins looked uptight again and said "I saw Butch just yesterday, he was upstream with his kid! What gall? That mechanic was fishing!! I was going to give him a few words but…"

"You were still too shaken up by Mrs. Markle to think," Fred teased.

All the men laughed, including Jenkins. Least he could laugh at himself sometimes.

Butch walked up behind Jenkins but didn't act like he had heard anything. He walked out the door and two minutes later my sister Kasie walked in, whistling.

"Here Mr. Jenkins," Kasie said as she handed him a note.

"Now what?"

"This is from Butch Gambill the mechanic, the one on First. I just ran into him and he said to make sure you got this so I am; it's a small

Murphy and Jenkins

list of other problems your truck has that better get fixed or you're bound to have even more problems that…"

Fred winked at her as he interrupted saying, "Looks like somebody's had twenty cups of coffee this morning."

"What'cha mean?"

"I'm just teasing you, having some fun kid. You are hyper, you talk faster than a fox on its way to an overweight chicken convention!" Fred explained.

"Ain't that the truth!" Jenkins agreed.

Kasie laughed, "I guess that's me all right!"

Kasie looked at Jenkins and spoke again. "He also asked if you've got time if you'd like to join him and his boy fishing Saturday at Lake Osborndale, you know the time and…he said it might calm you down if you fished again. He said he is taking care of your truck but he has to go it easy because of his heart."

"Doctor Andersons, that was why he was there? His heart? You were right boy. I thought you were kidding me!" Jenkins said, looking at me then at Kasie and continued. "I thought it was for migraines…yeah, guess this is our fishing Saturday, every first and third Saturday." Mr. Jenkins looked very sheepish.

As Kasie and I walked out of Tinti's for school, I had to shake my head at old Jenkins. But Kasie had her thoughts somewhere else.

"You think you'll eventually find foster homes for the chicks until the Henderson barn is rebuilt?"

"I'm sure Mrs. Henderson can handle it, the church is doing it now anyways."

"You're *so* heartless big brother!!"

"They're not my responsibility Kasie, the horses are. You know that." I spoke calmly in spite of my sister's excitement.

"Pastor John called Dad. You're supposed to help us move some junk out of people's attics after school. We might have some kind of fundraiser at the Green. Imagine a fundraiser Eldon, at the band canopy!"

"At the band canopy?"

"The one where the little spring goes through the park and the cherry apple blossoms are lining the trail. That canopy on the Green is off to the side of that very trail."

I rolled my eyes at her comment, saying, "I know where that canopy is Kasie, but who is going to get any bands here, and, whose idea is it to have a fundraiser?"

"Christine, she even talked about this to Pastor John to see about him organizing it."

"NO WAY!" I exclaimed.

"I know, everyone thinks she's a wallflower."

"To say she's shy would be an understatement...Kasie, I guess you'll be pretty busy then helping her, huh?"

"YOU HAVE TO HELP BIG BROTHER, besides if you want to ride their horses before summer's over maybe you'll think about helping out with the fund raiser too, Eldon."

"Whatever. I can ride Jake from the Holmstead's farm just as easily."

"They won't let you if you don't help out. I already talked to..." Kasie stopped herself, realizing she had said too much.

"Who says?" I demanded, getting no reply at all. Sisters can be a pain.

I didn't want to think about what Kasie was saying, because the farm could not be lost to us. There was just no way.

I was distracted by the loud crash of a falling clam. A few seagulls dived and glided in front of us, among the first I had seen this year. They were dropping clams right on the street in front of us. They also were dropping the clams on the rooftops of these shoreline homes in order to crack the shells open. The locals were accustomed to these sounds, and the various foghorns and whistles that passed by day and night. I escaped by thinking about something Christine had wrote in an essay: 'Is there anything more beautiful than the cry of the seagulls? What can compete with the waves and wind? Have you ever sailed in the wide open waters, or fallen asleep on the beach with clouds stretching above you, the warmth of the sun comforting you?' She thought just like an artist.

Kasie grabbed my shoulder.

"You're doing it again. You're lost out there big brother."

I looked to my left behind Kasie and could see dozens of small sailboats leaving the docks, and dozens more returning. It never stopped. There was always something happening at the beach. Some scampering creatures, a great variety of passing ships, an ever changing mood of skies and waves, if only you had eyes to see it. Kasie interrupted my thoughts again.

"You know what's funny about you, big brother?"

"What?"

"I remember you got in trouble for calling Mrs. Markle a moron, so you were asked to apologize to her and you say to her, in front of Dad, Mom and me: ' I'm sorry you're a moron' ."

"What's your point Kasie? I felt sorry for her, that's all."

"You were supposed to apologize, but... nooooooooooo... my point is once you see it's not so badddddddd, you'll help out, like later when you told us Mrs. Markle really wasn't as stupid as you thought she was and you even defended her from name calling!" Kasie was getting all hyper on me again, waving her arms like a crazed gorilla to express her ideas. But I was used to that.

"Kasie, I just don't like Balligrino, that's all, he's an idiot."

"Well, you need more to do in your spare time than going around town drawing stuff and daydreaming. People think that's weird, what ya think you're going to be the next Rembrandt? Get with the program here!"

"If you'll get off my case I'll help you and Christine with whatever you got planned later on. What do you got planned?"

"Nothing yet. But at lunch we're going to shop for a surprise for Mrs. Hophenetter, only I can't tell you about it. But we have no ideas for the fundraiser yet."

"That's just wonderful." I groused.

So that whole day at school I had that over my head. In between classes I'd run into Kasie, who was skating from one class to another, which was totally against the rules but I wasn't going to say anything to her about it. She didn't care if she was caught or not, because the teachers gave up warning her.

"Detention Miss Cooper," they'd say, but after a while they ignored her. She'd even skate on the stairs, wearing a motorcycle helmet of all things while we were talking. I don't mean she did this every day, but sometimes she just got kind of ornery. She did it about twenty-four times before this school year, and four times before she got detention.

Yeah, she was different, had her own style.

After school was let out, Christine chased me down at Old Salt's place called THE CROWS NEST; he was a Greek fisherman, who named his Fish and Chips restaurant after his childhood nickname. His hair even now looked pretty wild, curly and unruly. He had many different ropes cut at each booth, tied in different kinds of sailor's knots; he had old style barrels and many pictures of lighthouses all around. Over each booth was a net with carved painted wooden oysters, lobsters, haddocks, coalfish, sea cats and cods.

I liked talking to Old Salt, he would tell me a lot of stories about his life at the sea during the months of the fishing season, in the North Atlantic. He had just finished telling me another story, which I couldn't be sure was true or not. Then he all of a sudden started talking about some lady. "You know Eldon, I'm sure she loves me, but only for my money."

" Who Old Salt? Who is the lady?" I couldn't imagine who. I never saw him with anyone special. No lady ever stood on the docks to wave him off when he went out for weeks on end. The other guys had wives, a girlfriend or two.

"My lady loves me for my money. She's my fishing trawler."

I let out an audible groan.

"You joining us?" Christine asked, now besides me.

"Sure thing. He was just telling me about a storm they survived. And a lady."

"Another fish story huh?" Christine said, smiling skeptically.

"You better get moving young man, the lady has a mission!" Old

Salt was wiping a glass up at the bar. With his curly salt and pepper hair and trademark big grin, he was known to be quiet a popular character around town. He had forearms bigger than my legs, which reminded me of Popeye.

I turned my attention to Christine. She was carrying her violin case.

Why was she carrying a violin case? What were we doing? Where were we going? I wanted to hear the rest of his story, but I guessed it could wait. "Your uncle Jim's bus comes to the corner of fifth and main in about five minutes, Kasie is already there. We just finished shopping at Woolworth's for Mrs. Hophenetter."

Mrs. Hophenetter, just the mentioning of her name could put a freeze on a guy. I cringed remembering that strange hermit. Why did they shop for her? I complained about something else though. "Well, Christine, if the bus is packed he can't give us any free rides, so Kasie better not even think about that."

"No one said anything about a free ride, I have our bus fare ready."

"Oh…thanks…and sorry."

"Sorry for what?"

I didn't answer immediately, but waited. She didn't press me. After about a block of walking I answered. "My lousy attitude. Sorry."

" You should be sorry Eldon!" she teased.

When we got on the bus it was packed except for the back. Uncle Jim reminded me of Elvis Presley, the hairstyle and sunglasses. He loved the so-called king and Johnny Cash. He told Kasie to take her skates off before boarding the bus. "*Shava bree nopem lageno*?" Kasie asked.

I rolled my eyes. That game again. I had to translate for Kasie as if she were foreigner.

I told you my sister was unique. Or maybe she was just insane?

So I said "*Yukka de dena,*" I pointed to her skates and she took them off. She walked barefoot to the back of the bus, talking that gibberish all the way. I gave Christine a look like "What's going on here?" but she only smirked at me and answered with, "*Gabereen laden muck pavala,*" then she pulled out her violin. "Please don't play here Christine!" I whispered desperately.

Her eyes narrowed at me, and then she lifted her nose in disgust as she silently answered, "Don't be a shmoe." She once told me that expression only meant that and nothing else. My uncle Jim yelled from the front. "Eldon, tell the young lady to play her violin."

"What?!"

"Tell that nice exchange student to play her violin!"

Uncle Jim darn well knew who Christine was! Good grief! The others on the bus agreed, asking me to ask her to play.

So I said, "*Muckkka ree nue porkaloins.*"

"*Porkaloins*...Pork a lions." She laughed, saying, "Porcelain *porkaloins*!"

I motioned with the arms as if playing an invisible violin and Christine laughs, shaking her head in a yes motion, and says, "Ahhhh! *Pokalons*. Porcelains!"

She pulled out her bow and played. Most everyone on the bus got real quiet, including my chatterbox sister. A few guys didn't stop talking until they realized, hey, she can actually play that thing!

She was playing a variety of Russian gypsy pieces, blended with jazz and classical sounds. She was improvising. I can't remember the names now, but it was pure magic. I noticed a few people didn't get off at their regular stops so they could listen to her finish the piece. It was obvious she loved music; she threw herself into it completely but didn't lose her pleasure in playing it.

Even when the bus would brake, and she'd be lurched forward, she only messed up the notes a little, but her improvisational skills were such that it wasn't noticeable to anyone other than Christine really. When we got up to get off the bus, people clapped for her. She went to put our fare into the lips to the fare box, but my uncle Jim said, "I don't think they'll complain if I pay it."

We got to Mrs. Hophenetter's door. She was even stranger than Kasie. Her last year of teaching was when Christine and I were in second grade. She was a good teacher, don't get me wrong, she was just very strict and even then seemed terribly old to us. Most of our teachers were in their twenties. Here was a lady in her early seventies teaching second graders. Kids even at that age tried to take advantage of her, figuring her for a sucker. But she wasn't one to be toyed with. Those who tried learned cursive writing after school, or the multiplication table, even though the school board had said THAT was a full two years ahead of schedule and they said it wasn't allowed on account it might make us grow up bitter and we might not realize our potential. Which seeing all the fights in school, I thought maybe NOT realizing our potential was a good thing. But nobody asked me. I got pretty good in my times table after beating up Johnny Green during recess for calling me 'Chubby tubby'.

Go ahead. Ask me what seven times five is. That's the number of times she gave me detention that year. Which is also the number of times Kasie and Christine waited for me at the school library. After thirty years I can still recite those numbers. Since her teaching days Mrs. Hophenetter had become known as the "MIDNIGHT GARDENER", because she was known to do her gardening at night, in a miner's cap. Now that's weird, huh? About five years before this time, in 1972 she was found on the beach crying all night at Darboughry Point, she had walked the whole way the day of her husband's funeral. The police, including Christine's father, found her and sent her briefly to the state mental hospital. Christine and her mother used to visit her a lot. I knew that Christine's mother had problems just a year before that.

Emma Henderson, as Christine's mom was called then, was sent by her family to different doctors over the years when she was growing up, and even faith healers. Over a long period of time she got over her depression and attributed it to God and her faith. Her husband, Officer Solanski, didn't yet believe that one. But in her pain she was able to be a friend to Mrs. Hophenetter.

Anyways Christine was here, so at least I had some 'normal people back up' in case I needed to exit this scene. In case Mrs. H. asked me to recite my times tables in a miner's cap while digging for weeds.

"You the ones Pastor John sent then? Oh, I remember you kids," Mrs. Hophenetter said, sizing us up to see if we could do the work.

"Yes ma'am, we're the ones," Kasie said far too cheerfully.

Mrs. Hophenetter let us in and the sudden burst of cool air sent her seeking cover. Although from the outside things looked a bit run down in this Queen Anne styled cottage house, the inside was kept up pretty well. We walked into an immaculate Great Room, where plastic sheets covered the sofa and dressers. Everything was spotless. Mrs. Hophenetter sat in front of the fireplace on her plastic sheet covered sofa, Kasie and I immediately headed up the attic, and Christine played her violin for the elderly woman.

"She has dozens upon dozens of photographs, all bundled together in white yarn, Eldon, look at them!"

"What are we supposed to be looking for?" I asked my nosy sister, trying to give her a hint. "Think WORK SISTER! Not playing around."

"Think FUND RAISER ELDON... oh, look at these pictures! They got to be fifty years old or more! We need stuff to put on the fundraiser. Maybe..."

I would pull out some old junk that I thought could be salvaged and bring it to her garage in boxes... after getting a "YEA" or "NAY" from Mrs. Hophenetter. I waited for Kasie to help but she never did. I was getting irritated with her and said so.

"This stuff smells worse than dog breath and you're sitting on your tail."

"I don't have my shoes on Eldon. I only have skates."

I pointed to some old bowling shoes on a shelf saying, "I'm sure Mrs. Hophenetter won't mind, these'll almost fit you, maybe a bit big but..."

I never noticed when Kasie left the attic. I was thinking about how much I didn't like this work very much, it was too dusty, too dirty and smelly.

When I got downstairs for a can of pop a few minutes later, I noticed that the boxes of pictures that were in the cone cove of her attic were now all opened. There were photos on her dresser, on her couch, love seat, all over thanks to her helper. The opened bundle before Mrs. H. was from 35 years before. Kasie was only supposed to clean the attic of dust, clear things out for the sale, but the piles of photographs seemed to draw both her and Christine. Kasie could be a good kid as far as thirteen-year-olds go, but it seemed this always happened… whenever she was sent into attics… more often than not she'd retrieve some long forgotten teddy bear, a picnic basket filled with scrap books, a few oil lamps that looked like Aladdin's, and the poor unfortunate older lady or gentleman would be required to explain the history of the objects. However, they'd tolerate this as Kasie seemed so very interested in them, and she had our grandmother's gift for making a wicked cup of hot cocoa, which she now placed in front of Mrs. Hophenetter, and ran upstairs for yet another box. Certainly Hophenetter didn't have much patience for dawdlers; "How's it coming up there?" No answer.

She repeated the question only to hear "The labor is on us today Mrs. H., I'll have it all be cleaned up before we leave, I promise."

I sat down, as I didn't want to work for free. The elderly woman looked at me with a smirk, understanding why I sat down so quickly. She then turned her attention to the piles before her, where she was being sent back in time by the photographs. Sometimes she'd smile, sometimes she looked terribly sad.

"Life seemed fresher then, filled with hidden promises, but that was a very long time ago. Eldon, see Timothy's face, filled with that mischievous grin of his? He could fix about anything. I never put these pictures in albums. To think a lifetime went by and I never got around to it. I never really stopped to look at these pictures till today."

I decided to go upstairs and clear things out after all. It seemed Mrs. H. might get emotional on me and I wouldn't know what to say. It had to be a conspiracy to get me to work. I was soooo hungry too. After this Mrs. H. was explaining these piles upon piles of pictures to my pesky sister Kasie and her collaborator Christine. I overheard Christine asking Mrs. Hophenetter if she knew anyone who would take the baby chicks that were still at the Baptist church.

"I think I can work something out for you on that," Mrs. H. said.

"How about a makeover?" Kasie asked Mrs. H. "We went shopping for you today!"

Christine walked closer saying, "You have a very lovely face and I think we can do some wonders here."

Before she could say "No," Kasie had a ton of makeup from her purse lined up on the coffee table. Christine, who was brushing Mrs. Hophenetters hair, had joined her. I thought Mrs. Hophenetter would object, but she didn't. She made some terribly disagreeable faces though, but that was from Kasie's brisk method of applying makeup.

"For her skin tone she needs a light blush and powder. Maybe some frost over her eyes and mascara?" Kasie said, really getting into this.

"I love your waves Mrs. H." Christine exulted.

"You should talk young lady. You had those lovely waves in your hair when you were only ten years old. I remember your visits so well."

"Kasie and Eldon did the same for my mom the year before," Christine says, smiling. "Your face reminds me of a paper worn by kisses of the sun. The sun has looked on you kindly, your eyes are still beautiful."

"As if wrinkles were beautiful." Mrs. Hophenetter frowned.

"Oh, they can be. In your case," Christine paused a moment to check the look of the makeup. "You… who have wisdom absorbed into you like frost absorbs itself in winter on those lacy old oaks at Henderson's farm… your face has settled into a…"

"Icy cold old mug?" Mrs. H. said, laughing. I silently agreed with her.

"No, I remember visiting you as a child even. You were warm and kind even there in that awful place. Your face has settled into mercy," Christine explained.

"Let's go to the kitchen sink. I'm going to wash your hair, cut and color it if that's all right with you?" Kasie asked Mrs. Hophenetter.

The old woman smiled saying, "Can't hurt or break anything I suppose."

"Just a hint of brown. Not very much. I think I'll leave it on about ten minutes," Kasie said, then she looked to Christine for advice.

Christine replied, "Just put in some streaks for highlights in her hair. Don't cover all her hair. Her white is beautiful. I'll look at her outfits."

Kasie was feeling talkative. "You know Mrs. Smhidt was telling me about how Jason Sawyer just drives her absolutely crazy because he plays saxophone all night after his stint ends in New Haven. Mrs. Smhidt is our town gossip... his room is right above... kitty-corner to hers and sometimes this young girl sneaks up there, she is thirteen. She climbed up the vine trellis." "I don't like that kind of girl talk Kasie." Mrs. Hophenetter rebuked her.

"Oh no," Kasie answered in her defense. "I can't stand girl talk (just for the record). Not that kind of girl talk at least. It's not because it's bad or anything... unless it's sin... it's just that it becomes bad and ugly and disgusting when it becomes public. It's, of course, not the way it should be, since God created that relationship to be with only one person, a spouse, and that only that person knows how I feel about the whole relationship."

"You're going to wait for your husband then? Is that what you're saying?"

"Of course! Why include a person who's not even a part of that relationship? Sure, I'll probably talk about Mr. Right when he comes along, but I don't intend to ruin that special bounty..."

"You mean bond?"

"Uh... yeah... bond... that just him and I have—just for some girl talk, or bragging rights. So I'm modest, but I'm not ashamed of talking about this with my girl cousins, Mom and I. It's just I'd never spill my guts out to share my deepest thoughts and *Anne of Green Gables*-dreams about any matter with just anybody."

Suddenly my sister was blushing, realizing I was in the kitchen looking for a snack. I interrupted the talk with, "Got anything to eat, I'm starved." Mrs. Hophenetter pointed to some cold pizza on the counter. I grabbed three slices, and gave my sister a stupid face to try to make her laugh. I scarfed down the pizza in two seconds.

"What were you trying to say? You're confusing me honey. Before all this saving yourself talk, what were you saying about Jason Sawyer and all?" Mrs. Hophenetter asked Kasie.

"Well, that girl is only thirteen years old so Mrs. Smhidt would not allow Jason to take advantage of her, so she storms up there all ready to break out the canons, and she finds the girl on the keyboard accompanying Jason, with her older brother in the room. She asked the girl why she didn't come during the day… but I know why. Her parents hate music. They think it is of the devil."

"I used to teach music too, on the side. Who is this young girl?"

I knew who Kasie was referring to and interrupted. "Dad doesn't think music is of the devil Kasie, only at two AM he does when you try playing stuff."

Mrs. Hophenetter laughed and said, "Why don't you two… you three (Christine just entered the room with a beautiful pink floral dress in her hands)… come here for music lessons now and then? I can work something out on one condition. No night-time sneaking there and I'll get your music lessons free of charge by a REAL teacher… me!" Mrs. H. was beaming at us.

I wondered if Miss H. was coming out of her shell?

I told them "We got five other homes to work on so we need to get going Kasie, Christine."

"This is going to be soooooooo great!" Christine exclaimed. "Try on this dress Mrs. Hophenetter!"

"Well, first you need to wash that dye out," Kasie said as we left.

I doubted we'd have time left to do even one more home before supper. Yet we somehow did all of them. And like I said before, Kasie went crazy over pictures and knick-knacks at every house.

— chapter 4 —

Fishing with Jenkins

Now I already mentioned Mays Hobby Store, which had been in Apple Harbor for over 125 years… in one form or another. Before 1960 it was simply a men's clothing store with only a few toys for sale. It was always in the Mays family, but when Tim Mays the current owner took over he ordered more and more toys, plastic model cars, trucks, model train sets with every conceivable city… including an unlikely ancient Rome city with a coliseum. He had board games, jacks, marbles, cards, and rows of girl toys, a few bikes in the back… and one aisle for suits.

The wooden floor smelled of the oil used to treat it; the oak and glass cabinet in the front of the store had old coins for collectors, and the cash register itself was an antique. The ceiling was stamped copper, and was showing its age. The doorways had the antique style moldings.

But when I walked in the door that Saturday morning, I didn't notice those things. I saw Mr. Mays smile and heard his soft worn voice say, " Hello Eldon."

He worked the books and helped the customers and would order special medal models of trains for the adult collectors. His father had survived the great Depression by extending credit to the local people when his competitors didn't. The Depression hit Apple Harbor pretty hard, and it nearly bankrupted everyone. So Mr. Lee Mays, Tim's father lived off of an inheritance, extended credit, and after the Depression he flourished. People remembered that kindness and only did business with Mays. He never lost a nickel trusting people.

Mr. Tim Mays had a note hanging up from a young man who stole some toys, apologizing. It was right by the register. I couldn't remember a time not seeing that note there. It was dated October 3, 1965. The boy was now our sheriff.

I was here that Saturday to meet with Mr. Jenkins, Butch and Mr. Mays before they left for their fishing trip. It seemed like this was there second home besides Tinti's. I often wondered what adults had to talk about so much. They sure did enough of that.

On their way to the fishing they were talking about John Wayne movies. I helped them load their fishing gear into Butch Gambill's tan 1977 Ford F series pick-up truck. I wasn't going with them, not with Jenkins there.

He had a big mouth sometimes, and I had once jumped out of the boat and swam to the shore to get away from his complaining. I told them I wanted to leave because my legs were cramped, but everyone but Jenkins knew better.

"What do you think is the Duke's all time best movie?" Mr. Mays asked the men.

"*True Grit* without a doubt," Butch said with no hesitation. I helped him put the cooler in the back. He popped it open and handed me a cold Coca Cola for my effort.

" *TRUE GRIT*? Are you crazy?! What about *Big Jake*?"

Jenkins could turn anything into a life or death argument at times. Maybe that's why Fred didn't fish with him? I'm not sure. "Well, *BIG JAKE* was a good film, yes," Mr. Mays said, trying to ease the tension a bit. Butch could do a fair imitation of Wayne, and as he strutted up to the men I could almost see the Duke himself among us. Butch sounded just like him now. "I liked these quote of Wayne as Rooster Cogburn… 'I mean to kill you in one minute, Ned, or see you hanged in Fort Smith at Judge Parker's convenience. Which will it be?'; then there's his, 'Well, come see a fat old man sometime!' That's from *True Grit*."

"Didn't George name his quarter horse after *Big Jake*?" Mr. Mays asked Butch, who was carrying some gear into the pick-up. "I

CHRISTINE AS MIME

think so, yeah, that Henderson is a pretty decent guy," Butch replied.

I told Mr. Mays, "Yes, Jake is named after that movie."

"The Duke and I have the same birthday." Jenkins beamed.

"Actually the greatest star of all times would be Jimmy Stewart, now he could act." Mr. Mays was teasing Jenkins, pushing his buttons as they say; everyone knew he preferred Jimmy Stewart. He was an awful lot like him in personality. But he looked more like my ideal picture of a grandfather. He had a bushy white mustache, droopy crinkles at the sides of his eyes and unkempt white hair, which framed a heavy face. No matter how much he combed it the hair became a mess sooner or later, in contrast to his otherwise neat appearance.

Jenkins narrowed his eyes as he responded. "Okay, so maybe he's not the greatest actor of all times, but he's certainly the greatest movie star of all times, and the greatest American that ever lived!"

Butch and Mr. Mays looked at each other and stifled a laugh. But they couldn't hold it in. Jenkins sure took certain things very seriously. They laughed, but it was a friendly laughter, and it got Jenkins to smiling a little bit.

Now I didn't join them like I said; I only heard the rest of what happened that day from Butch Gambill, Mr. Mays and Mr. Jenkins. Their stories pretty much collaborated, except Jenkins forgot certain details that made him look bad. I guess I don't blame him for that. So they went to Gooseberry Lake, just outside of Hayfield, and Mr. Mays was really reeling in the Walleyes. He even caught a single large golden colored walleye, which I'm told is rare. It was pretty large for its kind I guess, and Mr. Mays figured it should be released. That started another round of arguments with Jenkins. But Butch photographed the golden walleye as Mr. Mays held it, then he let it go off the side.

"Catch and release is stupid, don't you think so Tim?"

"I've caught my limit anyways Ralph. It's no big deal. I catch anymore, we'll put them in your bucket," Mr. Mays said, smiling at Jenkins.

"I'd like to bag Old Charlatan," Butch sighed. He removed his garage cap to wipe some sweat from his brow, revealing a receding hairline on his tan head. It was getting hot out here already. Old Charlatan was a legendary large mouthed bass that fishermen had tried to catch for years. He was rumored to be as large as a full-grown man, and the story went back two generations. Although large men had snagged him, some of them with arms bigger than Mrs. Henderson's legs, no one had ever been able to keep him long. They say he knocked a man unconscious once with the kick of his tail. Fortunately the man had his lifejacket on. Only a fool wouldn't wear his lifejacket in Gooseberry Lake.

"You? You couldn't bag that old Charlatan with that flimsy line." Jenkins snorted.

"It's a strong enough line. With this ninety-pound line I could pull a yacht or go mountain climbing."

"90-pound line, yeah right Butch."

"Don't stand up in my boat Jenkins, it's dangerous!" Butch exclaimed.

"But I just saw something, a large shadow! It swam past… over there… I think… could it be that Charleton?"

"SIT DOWN NOW!" The two men yelled, Butch louder than Mr. Mays.

After a few more hours, Butch caught over his limit, but Jenkins didn't snag anything but underfed guppies. He blamed it on his bait, the sun, the line wasn't any good, it was too cold, and it was too hot.

The men were getting pretty irritated with Jenkins. More than they normally did I mean. But in order to be civil, between the times they asked him to not talk, Mr. Mays tried to make suggestions.

"Your tactics are too easy to see. They're not going to bite that stuff anyways. Not if you want…"

"Oh just shut up," Jenkins said to Mr. Mays as Butch reeled in another open-mouthed bass.

"Butch, what do you think of that Christine girl going around trying to raise funds for her uncle?" Jenkins was asking, his voice rich with sarcasm.

"So?"

"She's kind of a stuttering monkey I mean, eee… eeee… eee!"

"Like you don't stutter when you're nervous."

"She's a nice kid, maybe you should shut up," Butch answered.

Jenkins stood up again. He was pointing at a shadow of a tail again. It was heading straight for their boat.

"Put your lifejacket on NOW!" Mr. Mays tried to sound patient, but urgent all the same.

Jenkins did as he was asked. As he snapped it in place, Mr. Mays had turned to move the boat, and he made too quick a move of his elbow against Jenkins left foot, which resulted in Jenkins tipping. Then, something big hit them from the bottom. It hit very sudden, and very hard. With a flash of movement Jenkins was in the water. They saw a tail the size of their motor splash out of the water, and Jenkins' line fell in, dragged by old Charlatan.

"You pushed me!" Jenkins yelled at Mr. Mays.

He might have. But Mr. Mays blamed the fish Charlatan, and Butch blamed Jenkins himself for standing up. It was the last time they fished with Jenkins that summer. They figured he was too dangerous, too grumpy, and besides, he didn't have the money for a new fishing pole, as most of his spare money was tied up in that truck. It was probably a good thing that Jenkins lost his pole, because when the game warden came by a few minutes later, seeing a drenched Jenkins, who didn't have a license to fish, Butch could have lost his boat over that, but the game warden didn't push it. Without a rod, he didn't see it was worth pursuing.

"You better thank that fish or you'd be paying Butch here for a new boat," Mr. Mays told Jenkins later that night.

"Whale is more like it. I would have drowned if you didn't tell me to get that lifejacket on. I don't know what I was thinking."

When they finally dropped Jenkins off, the men felt freer talking again while driving.

"So, did you push Jenkins in?"

Mr. Mays just smiled. "I told him to put his life jacket on after he talked bad about that young lady Christine. I figured one of us would push him in, if not Old Charlatan himself."

"But did you? Tim?"

He never answered the question. He just smiled as he looked ahead.

* * * * *

After I left Mays that morning, Kasie and I did something kind of silly. We dressed up as clowns, the kind that don't talk (called mimes.) We got a grocery cart and went to Christine's house. You see Christine wanted to go to the library, and that involved a whole lot of walking, as it's clear across a bridge and then up these long high steps on a sharp incline, which went through woods up a hill. Because of Christine's ankles, she was going to get a ride from her mom. But Kasie wouldn't think of that.

"It's far too glorious and wonderful out here, it would be illegal for her to not enjoy some of the sunshine. We'll cart her over Mrs. Solanski!" Kasie said over the phone.

So, when we got to her house Christine at first objected, saying she didn't want to look like a fool. But Mrs. Solanski said, "Kasie and Eldon will look like the fools, that's what clowns are! Go with them honey." And to us she said, " Drive safely now, and take Yellow Bear, she spent the night here."

Christine climbed into the cart, which had extra large pillows and the front panel was removed so she had extra room for her legs.

She didn't talk, she just laughed now and then, smiled a lot and enjoyed the ride. A few passersby gave us grins, some looks of contempt. I spotted some kids from school who gave us very weird looks, as if to say, "You're stranger than Christine even!" But it didn't matter to us. We were having fun. Even Yellow Bear seemed nicer today; she ignored the cats that crossed our paths. With this kind of weather who wanted to bother?

When we got to the foot of the steep stairs through the forest, we ditched the cart in a spot I knew no one would ever look. We'd need to use it again on our way back on account of Christine's weak ankles.

"It's sure pretty through here, the way the light filters through these dark maples," Christine said smiling.

We just smiled back. We couldn't talk. It's against everything a clown-mime holds sacred. We looked more like circus clowns than anything else.

"I like it when you guys join me at the library, everyone else thinks it's weird," Christine said as she placed an arm around our shoulders in a hug.

We crossed the street from the huge gray stoned church, where the two lion statues sat guarding the entryway of the library. It was, and still is, a red stoned Library, built in the 1800s. It's a beautiful building, filled with large open spaces and plenty of room to lose yourself in books.

Of course, we tied Yellow Bear by her leash to a fire hydrant. She wasn't much of a reader, that dog.

The head librarian gave us all a funny look. We ignored her.

Christine went up the spiral stairs. She browsed through the medical section and pulled out several very large reference books, which I carried to a study area down that same wrought iron spiral staircase. Over the next three hours she studied, and wrote notes. It wasn't for homework. It was because she loved to study medicine. Absolutely loved it.

A little boy saw us, pointed us out to his sisters, and we smiled and placed a fingers to our lips whispering "Shoosh!" Kasie imitated the head librarian chewing us out, which made the boy laugh out loud. But he got the point.

It was an absolutely great day to be alive.

– chapter 5 –

Chief Smoky and the Crocus

On Monday Kasie went to see Coach Stein, who was the girl's softball coach for the better part of fifty years. She was planning on joining the high school team next semester, so she'd need to sign up now for training over the summer.

"I hear you roller-skate between classes in the hall young lady."

"Yeah… so?"

"You know that's against school policy. You have even gotten detention over this numerous times, yet you've chosen to disregard the rules. Why should I trust you to obey my coaching?"

Coach Stein stared at Kasie, not saying anything more.

"If I were to stop doing that…"

"What assurances do I have you can be trusted? There's more at stake here than just rules for rules sake you know."

"What?"

"Your safety. You're also compromising the safety of the students and faculty here every time you break those common sense rules. So what can we do about this so I can let you be a part of the team with a clear conscience?"

"What if I don't bring the skates to school anymore?"

"Not good enough Kasie . I know you could bring the skates in a knapsack and sooner or later you'd be sneaking off to skate in some hallway or other. No, I don't want that. I want you to skate. Skate to school. Skate in the courtyard outside away from others. We have a rink by the east parking lot. However, before the first class and up until your last class you are to leave your skates here, in my office, on my desk."

"That's crazy ! Leave my skates where someone can take them!"

"I know you're a great player, I saw you play for the Tigers last summer, but I'm not going to risk you being crippled because of some stupid stunt. Am I clear on this Kasie?"

She looked at him and noticed for the first time his right hand.

How many times had she seen it, but not noticed? It was deformed, the fingers were gone. He stared at her again, with a look that demanded the truth from her, but she also noticed in his eyes that he was an open man. His face was kind and his voice never betrayed impatience during this conversation. But she didn't want to give in just yet.

"How come no one else ever makes me do this?" Kasie pouted. "I know I got in trouble with Mrs. Supp and Mr. Danielski, but they never really… I don't know. It's dumb!"

He wouldn't say anything. She saw he was very patient, and seemed to have good reasons. She respected that.

"Okay, I'll bring the skates to your office tomorrow."

"You know if I hear you're skating between classes again, you'll be off the team."

"Yes sir. You're right."

"You are dismissed"

Kasie walked over to the bleachers by the softball field where my gym class was still playing the last inning. The score was tied, there were two guys on base and I was up. I had struck out twice and I wasn't about to let old Balligrino pitch me out.

"I'm going to knock this next one down your throat!"

I imagined myself hitting that ball clear to New Haven, being the hero as I meander onto home plate and the cheerleaders running up to me from the bleachers and… suddenly my thoughts were interrupted… the ball was inches from my face, I swung for all I was worth and the bat escaped my grip, spinning madly out of control into a free fall forcing the catcher to duck.

There are certain times in your life when you wish you could melt, fade, fly away from something you just know is coming. Even as my hands lost the bat in those split seconds before I felt the approaching thunder of rowdy laughter rise up within the bellies of the beasts among me. Betrayed! I saw my own classmates bent over into ridiculous fits of laughter, and the fact that our gym teacher, Mr. Gleasons was laughing too didn't help matters much. He was a man known around the school for his patience with the uncoordinated and uncool students, of whom I was king.

Being fifteen and not particularly good in any sport was very weird in Apple Harbor back then. At least I was no good when anyone was looking. Everyone, it seemed, was good at something. Even my sister, a year younger than me, had mastered several sports and could even brag about breaking her arm on roller-skates in third grade. She also fell out of a tree in fourth grade and re-broke that same arm. It wouldn't be the last time she fell out of a tree either, but that's another story!

The only thing I could show in regards to injuries was that callus I developed on my right pinkie finger from drawing. I was so glad it was spring. That meant school was almost over gym would be over too.

"Eldon, maybe I can pitch to you ? Don't want to end it like that,"

James said as he adjusted his cap.

It was then I noticed the field was practically empty, except for Kasie, Christine, James and Mr. Gleason.

"Sure thing James. Give me your best shot."

"This is softball, not archery."

I laughed at his lame joke. He was always cracking jokes but with James, people just laugh, there was something about that toothy grin and how he said things.

He pitched three curve balls and I hit two of them out of the field. I seemed to always do that when no one was around. Mr. Gleason wasn't even looking; he was chewing out that Balligrino guy.

Mr. Gleason was patient with us most of the time, but not when he figured you could do better. What could I do but laugh and heave a heavy sigh. He didn't even see my best hit of the day.

Whatever Mr. Gleason, whatever, I thought with a frown.

Kasie ran up to me laughing as she shouted, "News flash, local artist hits home run after the game!"

To which James added... "Future Yankees hitter Eldon Cooper was recently discovered by accident! His fly ball knocked out several in-flight satellites over the USSR, which really angered the Soviets. World War III is pending, but at least we got ourselves a BASEBALL PLAYER!"

I had to laugh. "Aw, get out of here you guys!" I guess it wasn't the end of the world after all.

"Hi Christine!" James yelled as she approached the field. We went out to meet her, leaving school.

"Hello James, Eldon."

"I see you're reading again. What... what now?"

"That's my Bible and this is *The Lion, the Witch and the Wardrobe* by C.S Lewis. Have you ever read Lewis before James?"

"No. But you sure like to read him."

"Reading books is like stepping into another time and having new adventures. A writer can speak long after he's dead to generations yet unborn."

Kasie looked at her skeptically, saying, "Unless of course the book is as dry as toast."

"Well, some writers have no life in them, just facts or facts they imagine.

James was the first to notice. "I see you got rid of your braces."

"Yes," Christine smiled. "Saturday afternoon."

"Smile?" I asked her. She did, revealing perfectly beautiful teeth.

We all "Ohhhed" and " ahhed", because it was a big difference. She had worn braces for so many years we couldn't remember what she looked like otherwise.

Kasie brought the subject back to reading. She said, "I'm sure you guys haven't read anything beyond comic books."

James tried to hide a book under his arm, but it was too late.

"What's this James? Oh, a book on Socrates, ohhhhhhhhkay."

She had a scornful look and rolled her eyes.

I shot Kasie a look that said, "Drop it Kasie!" and she did.

"It's something way beyond you Kasiebat," James explained. You see James was in special ed classes, some of the teachers just assumed he wasn't too bright as he stuttered whenever he got nervous, and also he didn't know how to read very well . He wasn't stupid. Teachers simply ignored him.

But Christine would occasionally find him a book to make him feel as smart as she though he was.

"That's a great book James. I brought you a book from the school library. It's on wildlife in Africa, see." Christine pulled it out of her book bag. "It has lots of pictures and shows their habitat and feeding habits, everything. So now you can go to Africa!"

"Oh, OK Christine, I'll give it a try," he smiled. "Where to now gang? Tinti's or May's Store? Food or STUFF?"

"Speaking of FOOD… if we weren't meant to have a midnight snack, why'd they put that light in the refrigerator?" I asked everyone.

"I'm broke James."

"You are always broke Kasie. You were never fixed."

I laughed at James' joke and playfully hit Kasie in the arm.

"Whatever," Kasie replied, rolling her eyes.

"Ewwwww! What a comeback. What a sharp tongue you got."

"Don't say it Kasie," I said, but she said it anyway. "Better a sharp tongue than a dull head."

To which James replied, "Could it be that God made woman last… cause He didn't want any advice while creating man?"

Seeing his joke fell flat with Kasie he added, "I'll loan you a buck or two if you really need it Kasiebat."

Kasie smiled in acknowledgment, as he handed her the money.

"How did you get that nick name 'Kasiebat' Kasie? I forgot," Christine asked.

"I pulled a James. I almost got three outs in the last inning, but I got a home run on the third try. So we won."

"So you three have something in common!" Christine gently teased us.

She was trying to remind me I also was a hero once too.

We had decided to stop at Tinti's then go on to May's. On our way we saw a bunch of Balligrino's friends harassing Old Smoky at the fire department. These kids were about as bright as a midnight sky if you know what I mean. If something destructive had happened in Apple Harbor, these guys were probably behind it. Balligrino himself had once stashed away his father's dirty magazines into the church hymnals, cutting out the centerfolds and placing them into the pages of the last hymn in every hymnal of the church. Fortunately Mrs. Henderson saw Mr. Henderson, who was five shades of red by now when he was dusting the pews. She cleaned out everything before disaster could strike. I had often wondered if Balligrino was related to old cleft hoof himself, the devil.

Now these guys had the old man surrounded like a pack of hungry wolves, yelling obscenities and mocking him, taking little bites out of him.

"LOSER!" one screamed, his face contorted in anger.

"I wasn't aware there was a contest," Smoky replied, cool and collected.

"Homeless hairy dirty old bum!"

"I'm hardly homeless, nor am I a shiftless bum, young man."

"Freak!" another yelled.

"I'm none of the above I'll have you gentlemen know, I'm a hobo, not a bum."

"What's the diff?"

"I don't scorn work. I'm a traveling man of the world. I can make the best hobo stew in the county."

Before we could do anything one of the rookie fire fighters approached the scene and broke up the kids. He was carrying some donuts and coffee from Tinti's in a bag. It was the rookie's job always to carry out the donuts to Chief Smoky. "Hey you cowards, I ever see you out here giving Mr. Franks grief again I'm going to bust some heads, you hear me?"

At the sight of this muscular large fire fighter they slowly left, mumbling and then acting as if they were now bored of Chief Smoky. I wondered who their next prey would be. They always picked on those they perceived to be weaker then themselves.

"What a bunch of morons!" Kasie yelled at them as they left.

"Be quiet Kasie!" Christine and I both said, nearly in unison.

"You all right Chief?" the rookie asked Old Smoky.

"Yeah Jeremy, I'm certainly not shook up by those kids."

"You sure got the fire trucks looking shiny today," Rookie said to Old Smoky. Then, to us, "He is very responsible around here, watching out for us, keeping an eye on our trucks and cleaning up any mess in the garage."

When we were leaving Christine was talking privately to rookie a moment and then to Chief Smoky. I heard her promise to mention something to her dad and she told chief she was praying for him.

"Remember this verse, Zephaniah 3:17 'The LORD your God is with you, He is mighty to save; He will take great delight in you, He will quiet you with His love, He will rejoice over you with singing.'"

Christine smiled her brightest smile and asked him, "You want to join us maybe Mr. Frank?"

He didn't want to at first protesting that he didn't take charity nor did he think we'd understand. She was very persistent, saying, "They got some great food there and it's on me. You just be our chaperone, our bodyguard, okay? From those guys. It's not charity whatsoever."

So he joined us.

"Christine!! Mannnnnnnn!! I can't believe this… errrrrg! "

"What Kasie? Hmm?"

Kasie was embarrassed to be seen in public with Chief Smoky, and Christine knew this, but she refused to acknowledge that fact. Kasie had made it well known how she felt about going anywhere in public with our Uncle Buddy. He had a way of humiliating us by going up to every single phone booth and checking for change. Or he would yell out so loud as he boarded the bus with us. "This is my niece and nephew!" He had a lot of ways to embarrass us without trying. So Christine was fully aware of how Kasie wanted to protect her image from being seen with strange people. Well, people she considered strange.

When we got to Tinti's, we went over the plans Pastor John had for the fundraiser. He was going to bring it up at the town meeting when the chamber of commerce's county commissioners had an open meeting. It was open to the public, but hardly anyone ever showed up. It generally got pretty disagreeable for most folks to hear what all came out of those meetings.

"What do you think Mrs. Smhidt will think of your idea Christine?"

James cut in mimicking Mrs. Smhidt's voice. "It's an absolutely horrible travesty of inhuman proportions. It's illogical even!"

"Irrational," I corrected him.

"Illogical young Eldon Cooper! Illogical!" James fired back in that Smhidt voice.

Our orders were placed before us all by Babbs, who was too busy to chat with us. The aroma of the food was intoxicating, and as Christine was talking I was eating away. "Well, I don't pretend to know politics guys. I just know it's right," Christine explained.

"Look Christine, you might have to get in front of people to present your ideas instead of Pastor John doing it for you."

"Yes, I know that Kasie, just change the subject."

"We all know that you dropped your speech class after your first debate. You wimped out."

"But I returned to the class the very next week, remember Kasie?"

"You don't have to do an oral presentation for two weeks. And you have someone up there with a chart to present your ideas like Pharaoh did for Moses." Kasie sounded very stressed saying this; I suppose she was trying to save Christine from embarrassing herself.

Christine laughed, "It wasn't Pharaoh... oh never mind, I'll still have to talk, more than Jennifer and besides silly Kasiebat, I have practiced in front of my Sunday School class. I'll be fine. You'll see."

James decided to try a joke to ease the tension. "Did you hear about the dentist and the carpenter who got married? Well... it didn't work out. They were always fighting tooth and nail."

Christine groaned, and laughed. Kasie ignored the joke and us; she was fuming. Her arms were crossed against her chest, she was looking out the window at Main Street.

Chief Smoky was really getting into his burger, fries and malt. But between bites he'd look at Kasie, then at Christine, then at Kasie again. Finally he said, "She'll be okay in front of people, give her some slack Kasiebat. And young lady," Chief was looking at Kasie. "And the rest of you are invited to have Hobo Stew with your families at the fire station. We can set up a time that's convenient for us all later."

"Well, I'll never turn down food," I said.

"We'll be busy." Kasie decided to speak for us all, still not looking at anyone.

Chief Smoky Franks snorted and said, "As you would say it young Kasie, WHATEVER."

"I say we go. I'm sure our parents won't object if they're invited."

"Thank you Eldon," Chief beamed, and added to Kasie. "If you're too busy flossing your pet gator or perhaps arranging your sock drawer I guess I can understand it Kasie Cooper. But you'd miss out on a great stew."

"Well, where you get the food from?" At this question even Kasie caught on she had offended Chief. "I'm sorry. I just..."

"It's alright. I get the beef from Weinrich Meat Locker, right next to Mays. I can assure you all of the food is healthy and safe."

"OK. I guess I won't be too busy then, I mean if our parents are invited and all," Kasie answered in a much softer tone.

"Certainly!" Smoky exclaimed.

I looked to the counter and could overhear Jenkins bragging... lying... that he had caught a walleye... "THIS BIG!" then complain in the next breath that his fishing partner still wasn't done with his truck yet. Fred was telling him about his grandchildren.

They were having two different conversations. I had to laugh as that happened a lot between them. I wondered if I'd be like that when I got as old as my fifties.

"The missus wants me to drop coffee. I can't do that."

"Why does she want you to drop it Jenkins?"

"I saw Doctor Sawyer yesterday and..."

"Well, doesn't that beat all? Isn't that doctor a lady?"

"My wife was the one with the appointment. I won't see no woman doctor, no. Cathy wanted her to check my blood pressure, that's all."

"And?"

"It was a bit high."

"Big surprise there, huh?" Fred said with a roll of his eyes, then seeing Jenkins' hurt expression added, "Well, anytime people go to see a doctor that's bound to happen."

Babbs came by, not hearing the conversation and asked, "More coffee?"

"Certainly!"

"No, make it decaf here for that pressure cooker." Fred was grinning.

"Pardon me?"

"Ignore him Babbs," Jenkins spat out.

"Well, what were you saying about the truck now Jenkins?" Fred asked Jenkins. Then, to Babbs he said, "This is great coffee Babbs! What's the secret?"

"It came from the bottom of three different cans we found in the basement, it's a blend of hazelnut and Amaretto and French Roast."

She yelled, as she was already on the other side of the dining area.

"He told me the truck needs new brake pads, the rotors look bad, the radiator is leaking and the starter is going out." Jenkins sighed.

"So, are you keeping the truck?"

"I think so. I don't know anymore. I think he knows about as much as my doctor."

"Doctor Sawyer? Your wife know about this Jenkins?"

"Doctor Anderson you wise guy. I figure if a mechanic misdiagnoses your car problems they should re-pay you for your time. The same with doctors."

"Face it Jenkins. The only doctor either of us wants is one that says to us 'Eat what you want, drink what you want and stay away from diets and exercise'."

"That's true. Doctor Anderson is getting pudgy and all he can say is don't touch this or do that and you need to lose ten pounds."

Over at another counter I heard a bit of a different conversation between Helen Smhidt and a few of her cronies.

Helen Smhidt: "Have you had any sightings of the 'Midnight Gardener'?"

Mrs. Doglas: "You mean that teacher?"

Mrs. Wallstein: "She had to give up teaching after that…incident."

Mrs. Doglas: "I don't mean to be nosy, but what incident? I'd like to better informed when I pray for her."

I had to laugh out loud; it was such an ignorant conversation to me. Everyone at my table looked at me oddly.

"What's so funny Eldon?"

"Huh? Oh, nothing James. What other ideas do you have Christine?"

"Finding someplace to hide if I get asked to talk in public."

"SEE! SEE!" Kasie says with a look of triumph.

"Oh honey," Babbs called out to Christine just as we were leaving.

"Make sure your mom gets these okay?"

She handed her a crocus, almost ready to bloom.

— chapter 6 —

The Crocus Blooms

The very next day in speech class Mrs. Robinson came into class late, looking like she had just gotten into a fight. Her hair was disheveled, and she looked very lost. But of course, Mrs. Robinson always looked lost. But what made this day so different was she walked up to the front of the class and said, "I want you to make a speech now."

Everyone looked at her funny, not knowing what she expected.

"Hello? Is there anyone home?" she asked sarcastically.

"Don't you usually let us prepare?" Katrina a cheerleader asked.

"Katrina, nice of you to volunteer."

"Bu... but..."

"You need to be prepared to think on your feet."

"I don't have anything ready. I thought we had another week."

"Say anything."

For the next five minutes Katrina got up and struggled to talk about her family, her boyfriend, why she moved here from California and then she didn't have anything to say. Mrs. Robinson told her she could sit down, and then asked Troy to talk.

Troy did better. He was pretty confident and found talking easy. Among the many things he had said was: "I want to give you my theory of the floating apex." Troy droned on. "It's whenever an organization has some useless individual who has risen to the level of their incompetence. They serve a new function, namely to not get things done."

Mrs. Robinson said, " Well, that's awfully cynical, don't you think?"

"It serves a practical purpose, namely to assign blame to someone who isn't really responsible for anything other than dusting their name plate on their desk. You'll see it in politics all the time, even here in Apple Harbor the mayor creates these committees, which serve no function other than to appease every little voting block possible. There's the Restaurant and Business Committee, the Farmer's Committee, the Ad council, the Sidewalk and Stoplights Committee and the Yankees Quitters Association, which is a front for grumpy old ladies to..."

"You probably better not let Mrs. Gomez hear that. She's only thirty and takes that club very seriously."

After about ten minutes more of this Mrs. Robinson asked him to sit down. Troy was brilliant; he was the first African-American kid to beat John Dalton, the son of Willis-Ragen School's principal, in chess. But he tended to talk above our heads, and talk on and on.

Then it was James's turn. He constantly cracked jokes while he was up there. Kids looked at him funny while he was telling these jokes, but not the kind of funny he found very encouraging. Finally she asked Rodent Rodney then Crystal Peters to get up. They both had a bit of a hard time with it. They stuttered and fidgeted, yet the class managed to survive their presentations. Finally Mrs. Robinson says, "Christine. Christine Solanski?"

"Yes ma'am?"

"Your turn."

Everyone looked and everyone stared. They wondered whether Christine would simply run out of the room. She had been known to do that before. Sure, she could talk to Kasie or me pretty easily, but never, never could she talk with any ease in front of her classmates.

She got up in front of everyone and cleared her throat. She looked up to the ceiling. I knew what she was doing. She was praying. She looked over at everyone and imagined the future. She saw Crystal in the year 1999 as a middle-aged woman talking to Renee Christopherson. They were sitting at Tinti's that by now had expanded somewhat, with a very old Babbs still waitressing. They were talking about Christine, pointing and sharing a laugh about that day way back in 1977 when she had stood up in Mrs. Robinson's class to make a fool of herself.

"Stop it! Stop it I say!" She yelled in her daydream. Christine then saw the scene change, suddenly instead of laughing at her the whole class, somehow transported to the future was cheering her on. She smiled at the thought.

When she looked up she saw some very placid faces. You couldn't wake these people up with dynamite exploded inside a fireworks factory.

"I want to talk about my grandfather. He had exceptionally kind eyes and his forehead showed no signs of anger, the sort of narrowing that gathers itself around the top between the eyebrows and forms hills of lines and sorrow..." She then pointed to her brow for emphasis. "Instead he had a smooth plain that lent itself to us grandkids, that we could rise up to meet him. The etching of the years only further burned that kind image in him, the dross of jealousy, cruelty and malice had been burnt out, leaving in its wake traces and shadows of fallowed beautiful skin. He wasn't perfect. But to us he was. After Grandma had her stroke he took care of her at his home, he could have put her in a nursing home as some social workers had asked him to, but he wouldn't do that. Mrs. Doglas really tried too. She's now in charge of child welfare or something.

"He could cook meals for a lot of guests and family, and he could cook for one, I don't remember any variation in his cooking. It was good consistently. Except I didn't like his beef tongue or pig's feet. One time my grandpa had cooked that stuff and we tried to pretend it was good, only our expressions betrayed us. He never asked again because we didn't eat it anymore after two or three bites, and we knew he felt bad about giving us that food, so he took us out to Rome Pizza in Hayford. It cost him lots to do that, but that was the kind of man he was. Uncle George and Aunt Betty had moved in to the farmhouse to help out, they had lived down the road but had always farmed Grandpas farm. They had wanted to help, as that was Uncle George's parents. So my grandmother was getting good care, and I never heard them fight but once, and that was just when they teased

Uncle George about his love for that biplane, and how crazy he flew it at times. I was on Grandpa's side of that argument. You've seen my uncle fly downtown.

"I remember how people in town would say 'Hello Mr. Henderson, good morning Mr. Henderson', as I rode on his shoulders. I was about six and I'd always say in a deep voice… 'Good morning Mrs. Markle, hello, this is my grandson', referring to my grandpa. He'd always laugh in that deep silky voice of his.

"I remember the way his face lit up whenever I'd show him a drawing, or tell him some story, or acted out something from a kindergarten play. He smelled of Old Spice and smoky oak that came from the potbellied stove; his hands were both soft and leathery from calluses and years of hard work. I'll never forget him."

When she stopped speaking she averted her blue eyes away from us all. Christine looked terrified, now her smile was gone.

Mrs. Robinson smiled as she spoke. "You've the heart of a poet and an actress Miss Solanski; see how you move your hands as you express the love your grandfather had for you, and the joy and pathos which shows in your eyes."

At that moment Christine returned her attention to the sea of faces, and like Peter who had stepped out of the boat, she was sinking. That choking feeling of the waters closing in on her became too much, and she ran out immediately before she drowned in those faces.

Mrs. Robinson looked weary and worn as she asked,

"Kasie, go check on Christine for a few. You got ten minutes."

Kasie, far too defensive, shot back, "Well, I don't even know where she went! I told her this would happen anyways."

"Check the girl's room young lady. And I mean NOW!"

Over the next few days Mrs. Robinson asked Christine to speak in front of the class. It seemed every time she would talk just a little bit longer, and she seemed just a bit less unfettered. But at the end of every talk Christine would blush and race out of the room. Of course, some of the kids found this terribly funny. They'd laugh as she struggled through her talk, then laugh as she ran out. Finally Mrs.

Robinson told Christine she wouldn't be asked to speak in front of the class anymore.

"I'm sorry I asked you so often," Mrs. Robinson said sadly.

"I forgive you," Christine said, teasing.

" Excuse me?! You forgive me?! I'm not sorry in that respect. I'm sorry that you haven't recognized your gift Christine. Maybe I shouldn't push you."

"I was teasing Mrs. Robinson. But… what gift?"

"Among all the kids, except for Troy, only you seem to have the natural gift for public speaking."

"Oh come on Mrs. Robinson! I'm the least likely to be able to…"

"That first day you looked up before speaking, why?"

"To pray for strength and wisdom."

"I'm by no means a religious person Christine, but if that helps you before you speak perhaps you should do that every time until you gain more confidence."

"I never thought of that."

"From your speeches, I gathered you love your family a lot, and animals. People were responding to that love and your passion for them… to you Christine… in spite of your shyness."

"I guess I never thought of me and speeches I mean. "

"So why did you take the class?"

"Because Kasie took it."

"Oh, her? She's a freshman, isn't she?"

"Yeah. You have freshmen through the third year in this class."

"I have a question for you Christine. Why ever did you take Drama?"

"Uh… Kasie took it so I thought…"

"That you should take it? Well, take it easy Christine, I'll see you tomorrow."

Kasie and I were waiting for her outside the class door. Christine walked out and said, " I need to do something. I need to figure something out so please don't say anything for a while, but I might need your help."

So we walked together in silence as she walked to the Drama class.

"Mrs. Kei? Mrs. Kei? I wanted to know if maybe you'd help me?"

"Yes Christine?"

"I want to… uh, well, I want to use the stage after school if I could?"

"What do you need it for?"

"It's hard to explain really."

Mrs. Kei could see that Christine was in earnest. She looked over at us and said, "I suppose they'll be needing the stage too?"

"Well, noooo. They'll be helping by… or rather be my audience."

"I'll be grading papers anyways. I suppose I could grade them there just as well."

When Christine stood on the stage she was very much surprised the spotlight fell on her. "Who's up there?" Mrs. Kei demanded, looking at the sound room.

We heard a shout from upstairs, "It's only me Mrs. Kei, Michael Kuncick, I thought you were having a practice this afternoon so when I saw her…"

(Kuncick sometimes worked the stage lights.)

"You might as well keep the light on her then." Mrs. Kei then asked, "If that's okay with you Christine?"

"Sure," Christine said, then looked over the stage and spoke out loud…

"My brother, my sister, although you're months from being born I can hear your questions to me already. The words are forming in my heart and soul like the etch work of snowflakes in winter, or colors being dyed into maple leaves. You'll ask me, I just know it… 'Christine, have you ever seen the glory in the sun-sprinkled morning when baby-faced daisies are first tickled by light?' I will say, 'Of course dear, of course.'"

Christine gave a wide sweep of her arms and laughed. "Then you'll go on with your inquisition… 'CHRISTINE! Did you ever roll on grassy hills, drinking in those stains like a puppy playing in her first snow? Roll, roll, roll, till sky and grass bluuuuuurrr together!'"

Then she rolled on the stage. Mrs. Kei stopped grading her papers and looked up.

"What, you wonder, accounts for my mood? My mother is expecting a baby! I want to dance and celebrate this life; I want to consider it. I imagine the joys and frustration this little one will bring us. Midnight feedings and first steps.

"You'll be demanding, I'm sure. I hope we grow in the process. What will you see? What will cause you to laugh?

"'CHRISTINE!! Have you ever danced a kite at midnight? OOPS, your kite got stuck in the moon again, now it'll be high tide as you pull 'er back home.' I know little one, I know. Then you'll wonder out loud. 'Christine? Ever ride a tire swing at night, those stars breaking your heart because all those celestial candles were lit for you? I have!!' You'll tell me, full of pride and joy! You'll brag that 'I swung so high I swear I could almost gather those stars in my arms…' So I answer you… OK, I think I will, one for tomorrow, one's for hope, and one for my heart, my sister or brother…you."

She is cradling a star in her hands. Or is it the baby she sees? We can see almost see it. As she's talking a few students gather in the assembly area. Christine is so caught up in her performance she isn't aware of what's going on out there.

"Your endless questions continue… 'Have you ever tightrope-walked across a rail fence, or mountain-climbed a snow bank? Have you ever raised your arms from the mast of an autumn glory-quilted maple… its leaves rustling its shimmering beauty?' OH! What an amazing thing this gift of living!! What secrets await you unborn child!"

You couldn't hear a sound in the assembly. Without realizing it, she had a growing audience of students and teachers who sat in the auditorium, numbers growing and growing. There were about thirty or more kids here already. The fact that they heard Christine's voice echoing through the auditorium drew them like a magnet. Their curiosity overcame them, and they came to see what was going on. Was this some new play? What is this??

Mrs. Robinson sat next to Kasie, Mrs. Kei and myself.

"Is this…" Mrs. Robinson asked Mrs. Kei.

"Yes, and no. I don't know who this Christine is, she's normally so… quiet."

Christine's strong voice echoed through the auditorium. "On that day when you'll be born… I can see it now little one… you might see the grove of trees all bare and huddled together like a disorganized choir at potluck. You see the winds flaying their mighty arms in praise to their Maker. You'll see a few stubborn leaves cling tenaciously to that elderly oak; in spite of the fury of the hill-swept spectacle, these leaves do not wish to join in that circle dance which most leaves make down our cobblestone alley. They have no sense of hurry, their sundials are forever eclipsed, they care not that winter is closing in. They simply cling. Just like you will cling to life itself. Your fingers open, your arms wide, as well as your cries!

"You'll see that rusted out rooster weather vane on Mrs. Rowe's farmhouse suddenly turn south… winter will bring its own brand of miracles. Geese, ducks, all gone, save for a few stragglers who'll miss the bus again."

Although it was spring she made it feel like autumn, when her mom's new baby was due.

"I wonder if Jesus ever felt this grateful for being alive? I wonder if He danced under moonlight with His brothers and sisters just because He was soooo happy?

"There is much more behind sunrises than my mere words can tell; there's a design behind every breeze-blown field that bows itself in composed choreography, a GENUIS behind the drawer of faces, who etched Himself into the beauty of souls that puts mere diamonds to shame… someday His glory in us will cause angels to blush, your light and life matters more than you can imagine little one… for we hold His GLORY in our souls! Imagine that! His glory in your soul!

"Yes now I hear Mom is having a baby. To you I give my heart little one…"

That was the end of that. Christine was shocked when those thirty plus students gave her a long applause. She hadn't even seen them having lost herself in that performance.

She didn't blush this time, simply curtsied, and raised a hand up.
"What was that?" Kasie asked, approaching the stage.
"Something I wrote two months ago, that's all."
"Christine. I want to talk to you," Ms. Kei said.
"That was really nice," Mrs. Robinson added.

— chapter 7 —

Christine's Assignment

"Yes Christine, I know this is an unusual request but I think you can pull this off. You'll have to think old," Ms. Kei said. "And don't worry about the realism. I've utilized the very finest in facial masks to create a very realistic look."

"It's certainly taking long enough."

"Three hours. But it'll be worth it."

"How's this stuff work?"

"I pick a mold to fit your face, then I apply the liquid latex gels. I apply a little make-up and voila! Photo-realistic mask."

"It feels like goop or jelly. You sure it'll work?"

"Don't worry, it'll be as hard as a rock in ten minutes. It works best in cool weather. On very hot days it won't stick very well. I was worried about your face with its high cheekbones, but this will work. You'll look really old soon."

"How… wonderful."

"That cold completes your voice too. Just raise it an octave, scratchier… you do listen to your grandmother? They don't talk as much as young girls. Hmm, also—you'll need a bit of padding."

"Padding?"

"So your body looks all worn and tired from being around so long. You have no figure to speak of," Mrs. Kei said.

Thanks a lot," Christine retorted. "I already knew that."

"Which means cinching under your blouse to hide your youthfulness won't be so tight. We'll give you these plastic teeth to wear; yours are too straight and white. And wear gloves, little white ones you see the old women wear all the time."

Over the next half hour, after her face was completed. Mrs. Kei gave Christine pieces of foam for her stomach and hips, a wig and old long dress and glasses.

When Mrs. Kei was done, Christine looked in the full-length mirror and was utterly shocked at the difference. It made her feel old to see herself that way. For a moment she couldn't say anything, just stare at the image before her in complete disbelief.

"What do you think Christine?"

"Wow, I can't get over it. That padding sure makes my tummy look floppy. Ha! Everything's so different. My face, my eyes, my nose, hair... wow, this is cool!"

"When do you want to start? "

"As soon as I leave the school I'm going to see Pastor Axworthy to help with the bell. We're just looking at it. I guess I'll start then."

Christine then left the stage area, and was surprised to see Professor Felix Mains leaving his office so late. He was a Professor at Yale as well as a teacher at our high school.

"Hello Professor Mains!" Christine said heartily.

"Excuse me? Who are you?" The professor was taken back by the sudden appearance of this old woman with a young lady's voice.

"Christine Solanski. I'm one of your students. I'm in make up and mask for an assignment in Mrs. Kei's class. How are you today?"

"Well Miss Solanski, I have to say it looks real enough. I was just going over some of the classes papers and wanted to ask you about yours."

"Yes?"

"The assignment was 'Do You Believe In A Creationism or Evolution.' Your arguments were very good Christine. I have to ask you now, this is not for a grade or anything but merely to satisfy my morbid curiosity... do you suppose this God of yours... does He care?"

"How do you mean this question Professor Mains?"

"There are four billion people overpopulating this earth and depleting its natural resources. What I'm asking is if God could care about an individual among four billion individuals."

"Yes, of course, look at your microbiology. There is evidence of a caring detail-orientated designer behind the molecular structures of everything. "

"Well, certainly I teach all that young... well, Miss old lady Solanski, but that only proves good order. He could have left the watch running after He left the shop, don't you think? Assuming there is a God."

"There is the heart of a parent behind every system responsible for our life. This earth is a prepared place for us by our Maker."

"Couldn't these systems merely be the byproduct of happy accidents Christine? A serendipity of sorts. "

"Don't patronize me Professor Mains," Christine said good-naturedly. "Random acts that lead to intricate order? If your worse behaving students got into a fight every day as you spoke, would that result in your classes being more harmonious? You taught us yourself that there are ten thousand genes crammed into the chromosomes, packed tighter than sardines or New York sub commuters you said. And further, you also said that these cells contain three billion subunits of information hooked into specialized DNA components of the protein. How can THAT be an accident?! "

"But that a God made it? That's a leap of faith."

"I see Professor Mains," Christine smiled and pointed to his watch. " You never ask yourself what accident happened at the watch factory to assemble your watch, yet how much simpler is it in design? As you should be led to concur, evidence of design concludes there must be a designer."

"For an old lady you're pretty sharp."

"I ain't buried me brains in Gloucester yet mister!" Christine said in an old lady voice. "Remember, as it says 'Job 26:7 He stretcheth out the north over the empty place, and hangeth the earth upon nothing.' The rest of the ancients thought the earth got hung up on a turtle, which hung on a frog, which hung on a log, which hung on an old lady who swallowed a fly, perhaps... never mind!!"

He laughed as Christine broke into singing that silly old fly song as she meandered down the hall. The Professor knew those old legends. This really gave him something to consider, he didn't realize the Bible had anything to it.

* * * * *

"Okay, so you understand my assignment Pastor John?"

"Certainly Christine, uh, what am I to call you now?"

"Debbie. My grandmother's name is Debbie so I'll play her, Dad's mom's maiden… oh forget it!" Christine exclaimed.

"In that get up you bear a strong resemblance to her. Helen won't know who Debbie is, nor will Buddy."

"Helen? Buddy?"

"Helen Smhidt and Buddy Lewis."

"Oh good grief! I know them… I can't…"

At that Christine went into a coughing spasm. There was a knock on the office door.

"HEYYY!! ANYBODY HERE? ANYBODY?"

"That would be…" Pastor Axworthy asked.

"Mr. Lewis, I know him anywhere." Christine sighed in resignation.

"We're right on our way out now, hold it a sec."

Pastor John grabbed the keys to the youth van and the four of them piled in, with the ladies in the back seat.

"There's just about enough room in the back for the bell with that final row of seats down. It should take us half an hour to get to Haven."

"Yes, but Mr. Axworthy, did you…"

"You can call me Pastor John, Helen."

"I'm sure I'd rather not do that."

Christine interrupted with, " You are Helen then?"

"Nice to meet you…"

"I'm Christine Solanski's grandmother, Debbie Andrews."

"I'M BUDDY LEWIS, BUDDY LEWIS!"

Christine resisted the impulse to say, "Hello Buddy Buddy Lewis Lewis."

"I'm here to check on the quality and tone of the bell. I'm the chairwoman of the Yankee Quitters Association here in Apple Harbor and my family has been involved in the railroad for years."

"Yeah, railroading people," Buddy grumbled in a loud whisper.

"I'm simply here to negotiate the sale of the bell," Mrs. Smhidt said, glaring at Buddy.

"That's true," Pastor John said, now recovered from Helen's earlier remark. "Her family owns the bells up in Haven that we'll be looking at. She also can tell the tones of the bells as her background is in music."

"Yes, I played the bells in the Christmas program at St. Anthony's Catholic Church last year." Helen beamed.

"Make a joyful noise unto the Lord, all the earth!" Christine exclaimed.

"Yes, well, it was fun I can say that," Helen managed to admit.

"I'M HERE TO HELP LOAD THE BELL, YOU KNOW!"

"That's wonderful Mr. Lewis. Certainly," Christine said.

Helen leaned over and whispered in her ear, "He's drunk."

"He stunk? Not really. My shoes smell worser."

Helen's eyes got really big.

"Or is the proper word worserest?" Christine tapped her chin, as she pretended to think about that.

"I don't suppose you heard about Arny Miller?"

"I won't hear it now either honey." Christine smiled.

"He went around two timing with that floozy…"

"TELL ME ABOUT YOUR GRANDCHILD… *COUGH, COUGH*!!" Christine got into another spasm.

Between her falsetto voice, her shouting and her coughing my uncle Buddy never heard who the floozy was. "Who was this floozy?" He kept asking.

Pastor John said, "No thanks Helen. Don't even think about telling us."

So Helen changed course midstream. "My granddaughter goes by my middle name."

"Which is?" Christine asked.

"Helen. I don't go by my first name. It's too hard for people to pronounce right. Helen was just so much easier"

"What does she do, your Helen?"

"Anything she puts her mind to doing Mrs. Andrews."

For the first time in her memory Christine could see Helen smiling. She knew Helen was the butt of many jokes around town by men who saw her as the reason for their marriage troubles. Helen's Yankee Quitters Association was known around these parts for the many marriages it destroyed. A third of the women there were divorced within two years of signing up. Which is why some men insisted their wives find some other activity to attend. Christine's own mother quit after three weeks because she said it was entirely a man haters' club.

Which conjured up some memories. Christine remembered her mother crying, the shrillness of her mother's voice as she came home from one such meeting. How she had wanted to comfort her mother that day, but she refused comfort until she cried out… "All they do is talk dirt on the town and each other, when someone misses a week because of a sick child or some pressing business… why they're like a pack of vultures tearing at the lady, but let her show up and it's all sweetness and light. I HATE THAT PLACE!"

She remembered her mother's tears as she held her that day.

She tried to dismiss the thoughts. "Lord, I sure could use some help here," she prayed wearily in her thoughts. "I don't want to hold that against Mrs. Smhidt."

"Tell me about your husband."

That was the first time Helen was quiet. Then she replied, "He's gone, dead."

"I'm sorry Helen." She meant it.

"Cancer."

They let the road pass by for a bit, the two feeling uncomfortable with the way the conversation had turned. Both of them were wrapped in Helen's sorrows. She distracted herself by thinking of Mrs. Lewis, my grandmother, and all the silly songs she had sang for us. She thought of how the corners of her eyes drooped a little, how lines wrapped themselves around the corners of her mouth into a nearly permanent smile. She thought of her hands, so knobby and tight, how the skin folded over her knuckles into those elongated fingers. She remembered how those fingers felt when they prayed together, or baked together, or how bright her eyes looked.

"What do you hate about being old?" Helen managed to ask finally.

"Hate?" Christine thought of her own grandmother, and the complaints she used to sometimes make. Then she thought of the old ladies she saw at the nursing home.

"I guess," Christine sighed. "I feel pretty blessed. Sometimes my fingers hurt and my knees swell but I'll be all right."

Her fingers and knees were swelling as a matter of fact. Christine had juvenile arthritis among other health problems.

Helen's brow furrowed very deeply as she began to speak.

"I hate everything about it. The punks who knock on my door at night just to harass me, the pain in my back, and losing my friends every year," Helen said, punctuating it with a curse. "Oh, pardon Mr. Axworthy."

"Sorry you're going through that," Pastor John said simply.

"You're not that old yet, young lady," Christine replied.

Helen smiled a little. "I'm sixty-six. I feel like a dinosaur."

"Next time those kids bother you at night, leave them some gift certificates for Tinti's."

"Excuse me?"

"Then invite them in. I think they'll either enjoy your company and leave you be or they'll get bored of you. You'll be keeping them out of worse trouble in any case. You'll lose all mystery so they will seek out new game."

Helen appeared to be considering her suggestion. After a while, Christine pulled out her Bible, the trip was getting long.

"I suppose you really believe that stuff."

"Yes, don't you?"

"Are you one of those born againers?"

"Yes. Call the police will you now?" Christine didn't let the kindness leave her scratchy worn voice.

"I'm sorry, is it Debbie? I shouldn't talk like that. It just strikes me as odd, that's all."

"I love Jesus Christ, He's my Savior and Lord."

"I'm glad you found something that works for you."

Christine nearly laughed out loud at the thought that Jesus Christ was merely something that "works for you." Like any other choice really. A choice between pickles or the Savior, fries or faith.

"What do you believe Helen?"

"I don't think I can answer that in so many words really."

"I wondered what you have to hold on to through the storms?"

"What are you reading?" Helen asked.

"The Psalms."

"My mother loved to read to me from the Psalms as a child.

It's funny, I can still remember her favorite verses."

"Yes?" Christine asked her, coughing again.

"Trust in the Lord with all thine heart, lean not unto thy own understanding, but in all thy ways acknowledge Him…The Lord is my Light and Salvation, whom shall I fear… and… I will sing of the Lord's mercies forever, with my mouth, I will make known thy faithfulness to all generations." Helen said this very softly, as if betraying a secret.

"My mother's favorite verse, John 14: 19, 'Because I live, you also will live' and I like the prophecies of the Messiah found in Isaiah. If you've ever read the Psalms…"

"Yes, love them Debby."

"All the psalms. David poured out his pain to God throughout."

"God helps those who help themselves. We can't cry to Him every time…"

"That's not in the Bible Helen. Rather He takes the weak and foolish things of this world to shame the wise."

"Let me see your Bible… I need to find a verse." Helen grabbed at it. And Christine recited from memory. "There is none righteous, no, not one. There is none that understandeth, there is none that seeketh after God. They are all gone out of the way, they are together become unprofitable; there is none that doeth good, no, not one." (Rom 3:10-12)

"My opinion is this," Helen reported. "The Bible is sometimes negative about people. Some very uneducated shepherds wrote it during a dark time of history. People are basically good now so I'm sure in the end God will forgive everyone."

"Where'd you read that? In a greeting card, or maybe the book of Denominations?"

"Where's the book of... oh, you're teasing me."

"Yes, I am. I heard a story about an American touring the desert of the Sahara. He was wearing a bathing suit and running towards the ocean. He saw a shepherd whom he asked where the ocean was. 'Oh, it's 800 miles away!' to which the American responded, 'Ah, what a beach!'"

"Oh no! He'd never make it!"

"Neither would we on our own. Simply read the Bible for yourself to see who the actual author is. Over 66 books written over 1500 years with a single theme, God's restoration of mankind."

"Interesting. I never thought of that Debbie."

"You know that child Kasie Cooper? We were talking about what pets we'd like to have in the millennium. That's when Christ rules the earth for a thousand years, where the lion lies down with the lamb. You know, I expected her to say she'd want a bunny or a pony, but she said 'Ohhhhhhh yeah! I want to pin that brachiosaurus to the ground!' How did she say it... 'That old necky dinosaur!! Ha ha! And I want to wrestle lions and tigers and bears'"

"Oh my," Helen said, laughing. "Lions and tigers and bears."

They both shared a laugh at that remark.

"She went on to say 'Ahhhhhhh, yes! Swim with dolphins too, and race with horses, fly and dive with eagles and... wow!' Well, you understand. She was quite exuberant about it."

"I'm going to have to read my Bible more I guess. I was never aware of a merciful side to God, never mind a fun side," Helen remarked.

When Christine left, she forgot her Bible. Helen grabbed it earlier when they were talking, wanting to look up some verses. Helen didn't notice it until later that evening at her home, when she saw it next to her purse. She opened a note folded in the Bible that Christine had written.

Hi Kasie!

I want you to remember that God places a very high value on your life and heart and mind. He sees the qualities that He put into you, and regarding the pain, your problems and shortcomings in whatever, God will certainly not judge you harshly or anything. On the contrary, He will build you up and all the hurts will be burned up like dross in a silver smelt-kiln. God is for you. Always always remember that. He is your Daddy, happy at your victories, delighting in your wins!! Don't be too hard on yourself, OK, because it's a false picture of who you are in Him! You are loved and cherished by Him sooooo much. That is one of the delights of heaven, we will finally recognize true greatness that is within the IMAGE OF GOD that He put into each of His children, put there by the cost of His Blood. He has a special purpose for you. It is His delight to see it unfold...

Romans 8:18 "For I reckon that the sufferings of this present time are not worthy to be compared with the glory which shall be revealed in us. For the earnest expectation of the creature waiteth for the manifestation of the sons of God. For the creature was made subject to vanity, not willingly, but by reason of him who hath subjected the same in hope. Because the creature itself also shall be delivered from the bondage of corruption into the glorious liberty of the children of God. For we know that the whole creation groaneth and travaileth in pain together until now. And not only they, but ourselves also, which have the firstfruits of the Spirit, even we ourselves groan within ourselves, waiting for the adoption, to wit, the redemption of our body."

In Christ your happy sister,
Christina.

Here's a poem I wrote!

BEFORE

Before He stretched out the heavens upon the
Black velvet canopy of space adorning them
Extravagantly with every precious gem
He knew you
He loved you
Before this old globe was teeming with abundant life from
His vastly complex mind
Great dinosaurs and monarch butterflies
Dolphins and swallows
In His hand a mark, a scar
I see He's written your name there Before there was
dance, light, or time
As He laid earth's foundations
He dreamed of the day where you both could celebrate
together... alone
He spoke world's into existence
But as far as you're concerned..
He stopped... paused... took His time
"One of a kind, a child of Mine!!"
He bore your shame and understood your grief
He knows what makes for REAL LIVING
This LION, This MAN... This KING
He never wanted you to be alone
He understands EVERYTHING in being you
And gave up His crown to win you over
To life"

Helen laughed reading this note, and grinned from ear to ear. "Now I know where Christine got it from…"

— chapter 8 —

Balloonist

Now the following week Christine was given the assignment of dressing up as a Mime, and not being allowed to talk for a full thirty hours.

"I want you to watch people Christine. You don't always have to perform, but you should learn to absorb as much as you can," Ms Kei had explained. That wasn't really that hard of a task for her. She simply waited till the weekend to start.

We tried every approach to get her to talk, the sneaky approach, the sideways approach, and the bold approach. None worked. I resigned myself to the fact I'd have to hear a lot of Kasie this weekend. So I called James over to join us at the Henderson's farm for my sanity's sake.

"Well kids," Mr. Henderson smiled as he spoke. "I was thinking today would be a fine day for flying. Who wants to join me?"

Of course we all wanted to, but as there was only one seat more besides the pilot's, we'd have to take turns. James went first. Then Kasie. Then me. I loved it. Although it seemed we had to fly awfully low. Then he would slowly ascend until we could see all of the farms of Apple Harbor below, the creeks, over the beach where we could see Long Island Sound with its tugboats and tiny waves. Then, he came down again. He did a few barrel rolls on his way down. I nearly lost my breakfast there until he got the biplane leveled out again. My knuckles were white, that's for sure.

I saw a balloonist heading towards the farms. He was caught in a down draft and was firing the balloon up again. There wasn't much we could do from up here. Mr. Henderson circled the balloon but then headed out for his own farm.

Then we flew so low over Main Street I could see the windows of Tinti's shake as we passed by. A small truck was driving down Main and I recognized it was Mr. Jenkins' truck by the rust spots in the hood. With a sudden jolt Mr. Henderson pulled up a bit. The truck screeched to a halt to avoid colliding with us.

"That was Jenkins!" Mr. Henderson yelled. I could hardly hear him over the sound of the engines rumbling. " I bet he has something to say about that!"

"He won't be alone Mr. Henderson!" I yelled back.

Now you're going to probably wonder how I know this part of the story, so I'll tell you right out... Mr. Jenkins told me. When he saw the biplane dive at him and he slammed on the brakes, they initially stopped his truck all right, they slammed everything he had in the back of the truck into the front, including his groceries and an engine he assumed was tied down enough. It wasn't. When the engine meet up with his eggs and milk, and a separate bag of glass he had packed from Nelson's, it made enough of a crash and a loud enough bang that he knew he better not look. He parked in front of Tinti's but then the brakes went out completely, he could feel it rolling so he hit the parking brake real hard and went into Tinti's to call Butch for a tow, and calm down a bit.

"He's re-living that day Parker," he said, as he sat down to retrieve a dime for the call to Butch's Auto Repair. Babbs gave him his coffee black.

Now, back to us... once we landed and were safely to a stop Mr. Henderson idled the engines and checked for leaks. He completely checked and re-checked everything over.

"Eldon," Mr. Henderson said. "You need to call the sheriff. That balloonist is in some kind of trouble the way he's flying out there right now. Christine! Your turn. No stunts though. We're checking on a balloon."

She looked happy knowing they weren't going to be doing any stunts. I doubt she would have gone up otherwise.

In less than a moment they were up and out of there.

Christine told me that particular flight was her first time in her uncle's biplane. She flew with goggles on, which smeared the white of her mime makeup and her curly dark hair was flapping in the wind. When she looked to the farms, everything looked so small, the various fields converging into my grandmother's patchwork quilts in appearance. She couldn't believe this was real, it was glorious up there, she had never imagined flight to be this wonderful. She could feel every rise and bank of the craft, it almost seemed as if she was in flight herself, free of all constraints.

The engine sputtered and shuttered, Mr. Henderson yelled something Christine couldn't quiet make out, then he pointed left. There was the balloon. She could see the balloonist, clearly looking agitated. Mr. Henderson was flying much too close. A balloonist here, imagine that! Christine loved the colors, it was a bright red and yellow striped balloon; it certainly didn't look like it was in trouble to her, just going into a landing. But her uncle had said this man was in some kind of trouble; but what could they really do about it? They had only a cheap radio for communicating, and that could hardly be heard over the sounds of the engine and... her thoughts were interrupted because suddenly her uncle went into a tight bank, making a very sudden and risky ascent to avoid the balloon.

The engine seemed to not compensate for the sudden demand on it, she heard a snap and saw smoke come from the propeller, which had seized up.

The stillness of the craft startled Mr. Henderson. It was unearthly quiet up there, just the winds slowly catching the drifting biplane. She hurried a prayer up without having to embellish it; she simply said,

"Daddy, looks like we're in a bit of trouble here." When Christine looked to her right, she saw a very bright flash of light come in from her peripheral vision, then extend to the engine and it started again, but it didn't at all sound normal. They had to limp to the airstrip. But we didn't know they were in trouble. We had left for the farmhouse to hear the scanner, and I was making a call.

I called the dispatcher who relayed the message to Officer Solanski while we were on the line. Mrs. Henderson turned on the police scanner, which was also used for weather emergencies. We heard some familiar voices cracking over the airwaves.

"Yes, I just now got word the balloon destroyed the Wallstien's cow fence."

"We heard," Mr. Solanski said.

"Hello, 911? I just saw this balloon making some kind of drug drop! You better send in some squad cars right away!"

"What's the last location of the balloon and the dropped bag?" the dispatcher asked the caller.

"On Interstate 5, heading out for Mariner's Drive. Those are drugs I tell you! You better get over there FAST!"

" You copy that car 72? Frank??"

"Copy." (We could feel his eyes rolling in that "Copy.")

"Margie, we need you to pass this along to the local four counties and the coastguard. That balloon is in serious trouble."

(Margie was a dispatcher from Hayford County.)

" I got it hon."

"MY cows!!! My cows just escaped!"

It was Mrs. Wallstien talking to the same dispatcher.

"We'll have to get back to you Mrs. Wallstien, I have five counties tied up in pursuit of a runaway balloonist. He's heading out for sea."

"I better not lose my cows or you'll lose your head!"

"Well… just CHILL OUT BABY!"

Even Mrs. Henderson laughed hearing that on the scanner,

"Sounds like that Dorothy Schulz, she needs a break!" she said.

When Officer Solanski arrived at Interstate 5, he took an educated guess that the winds would push the balloonist further east and eventually into the Sound. He drove in circles, trying to spot the balloon. Then he drove past the Lighthouse Darboughry Point and the harbor. He finally found the balloon, crashed in Crescent beach with five squad cars pulled up, their lights flashing.

Three of the police had their guns drawn.

"I doubt that's necessary Davis, Bacote… Cafaro. He's not going anywhere."

They still wouldn't put the guns into their holsters until Officer Solanski and two of the other officers explained they had better help the man get out of the craft because, "This thing can sink in less than a minute with that balloon deflating like that."

After about a few minutes of heaving and ho-ing, they were able to pull the balloon to the shore.

"You have been dumping drugs mister?" Bacote demanded.

"Drugs? What drugs?" The gray-haired man looked confused.

"The bags!"

"Those are for releasing my balloon you moron! I let out sand bags for lift, because I was got caught in a nose dive and crashed into a fence about a half an hour ago."

"Why didn't you stop after hitting the fence?" Officer Cafaro asked him.

"How? I don't have breaks. I was going too fast to stop in that field safely and there was a crazy biplane doing the vulture everywhere I looked."

"That would be my brother-in-law, George Henderson," Solanski sighed. " Yeah, I just got a call that he did a dive on Main Street."

"Where you from?" He asked the balloonist.

"I'm from Duluth but took off in Albuquerque, New Mexico with five balloons. There are two other hot air balloons in the area, we were all together until we got somewhere over Casper Wyoming. We were practicing for the show this summer when we got pulled in by a southeasterner. This must be Minnesota? Lake Superior, right?"

"No. You're in Connecticut. You wouldn't have wanted to cross that, uh... lake. Now hold it a sec here, were you just saying there's MORE balloons with you?"

"That's not Lake Superior... you mean?" and when he saw Frank's police car with its markings he laughed out loud... "I'm near my brother's town of Apple Harbor?"

Bacote yelled, "SOLANSKI! SOLANSKI! We just got word there are cows blocking traffic on I-90. We're out of here. That balloonist is YOUR problem."

"I guess you'll be joining me for a ride Mr.... Mr....?"

"Hal Parker is my name. Parker."

When the gentleman went to the front passenger door, Solanski apologized and explained. "Sorry, I can't let you up front. Rules."

Hal smiled, bemused. The name "Parker" never registered with Officer Solanski.

"Dorothy, this is car 72 reporting off Mariner's Drive just east of Darboughry Point, heading towards I-90. I understand there are two other hot air balloons in the area? Where's the traffic situation with these escaped cattle?"

"Closed off all Haven exits. All of them. The two balloonists landed safely in a field, one in Peter's field, the other in Wallstien's."

"Just across from each other then. Glad they didn't hit the beach too. Did you say ALL the Haven exits?! That's quiet a back up of traffic!! Please send word to Butch to tow this balloon off the beach at Darboughry Point... using his pick-up and hoist. He'll need to rope it in good. I'm heading up north to get the traffic under control."

"Be advised car 72 that there are four cattle cars in the area with dart guns."

"I copy that."

"Three of the cows have already been apprehended."

"Apprehended? Excuse me? Repeat please."

"You going to book them get their photos and hoof prints?"

Christine's dad could hear the dispatcher laughing.

"You got it."

All but one of the cows was recaptured within an hour. That last one, Missy turned out to be a real problem. She hid pretty well in the underbrush and woods surrounding Hayford. There was a lot of excitement on Monday morning when she wandered onto a schoolyard and started feeding on the nice green grass. The teachers couldn't maintain order in some of the classes.

They called the police but by this time Missy had left for greener pastures, those pleasant little green lawns. Several of Hayford's police... Cafaro, Bacote, and Davis... tried to capture Missy, but they had absolutely no clue how to do this. They'd chase her between yards; they'd run into hedges and woods. She jumped a five-foot fence, cleared it. The officers couldn't do that. "What the… is she some kind of deer?" Davis complained through labored breaths.

So they lost her again. Once again traffic was backed up along the interstate as Missy ran down the highway, right into traffic. That upset the afternoon commute for some drivers, believe me!

Two days later the Wallstiens saw Missy in their field. No explanation could be accounted for her reappearance. Perhaps she had hitched a ride? No one could figure out how she had come through a closed gate. Or if she had wandered on her own, how did she find her home? Some things are not meant to be understood. As Mr. Wallstien had explained his opinion on it… "There's just some things you'll never get a handle on."

About an hour after Mr. Henderson and Christine had landed, he was still going the engine over very carefully with his tools and making adjustments, trying to figure out what had happened up there.

"That flight was sure fun Kasie. Even if I did blow it being quiet today," Christine said, laughing from sheer relief.

Her mime make-up was a disaster. She asked for and received a face cloth from her aunt, and some cold cream to wipe it off.

"I guess you had a big enough scare though honey child," Mrs. Henderson said.

"Oh yeah! That was something!" Christine exclaimed. "Especially the very bouncy landing I hope NEVER to repeat!"

Now she was almost herself, except for a stubborn halo of white around her hairline. The shadow of a cross stayed on her right cheek.

Mr. Henderson was inspecting the belt to the propeller, having finally noticed the obvious. It was hanging there by a thread, all chewed up.

"I wonder how this could have happened?"

"Stress on the engine maybe?" I suggested.

"The belt's new, I just replaced it!"

"We're done here Uncle George?" Christine asked Mr. Henderson.

"Yes Christie, you kids go have yourselves some fun."

We left the field and headed down the road towards downtown. Kasie was feeling like a chatterbox as usual. Nothing new there.

"You know, about the time I was twelve Eldon thought it would really be a good idea for us to sneak out at night. Hmm. He had tried all day to cheer me up when Mrs. Solanski was in the hospital that time, remember? Anyways… he said we were to go to the lake on that rickety old raft. "Sure thang," I says, so we did. It was a summer night and I remember how awfully scared I was because we were riding our bikes through the cemetery, why I imagine all sorts of dead things coming for me and I was of a mind to tell Eldon off!! But, I look up at the moon, all silvery and alive, Eldon says,"Look the mysteries of heaven make the trees billow and blow." I know, sounds corny, but when no one's around he can be poetic.

"Yeah, I know he can be." Christine beamed.

"Corny you mean?" James asked, laughing out loud.

Kasie ignored him. "I forgot my fears and rode on. I fall exhausted on this raft, he just saunters like a cowboy, as if we only rode a few feet. 'WHATEVER ELDON' I said. I look at the sky all velvety like, and that big old happy shimmery moon, wow! He tells me a story he made up for me… then, all is quiet, even the frogs and crickets are still. The mystery permeated us, to speak would break the spell."

"What spell Kasie?" I asked her. She was sounding awfully corny to me too.

"The one God sent to cheer me up you lug head! I knew God and you loved me, even if you can't say it big brother. I remember biting my lip so hard because I did not want to cry even though I did. Kind of silly. Kinda nice. He hides the raft in some bushes, and I see these well muscled fairy tale oak trees lining the trail, with such a sweet heady scent of pine mingling among us from that grove overlooking my valley."

"Yeah, I know that grove," Christine said, smiling to encourage Kasie to go on. "That scent can waft down to beach some days."

"I have rights to that valley too you know," James said. "Don't go hogging it all now or I'll sue you."

Again, Kasie ignored him. "Intermixed with scents of lilacs, lavender, and sea-salt, yes, it was really nice. 'Tis the quiet scent of early summer,' Eldon was saying. 'Cuz the golden songbirds and ducks, geese, all raised their young ones so nature celebrates… see'. We fell asleep in this old rickety tree house, me in a hammock, (this was just on the end of Henderson's property), him on floor. Wasn't that nice that was of him? We slept past the alarm because he was telling me stories way into the night. I avoided a beating because I worked at this, the Henderson's ranch even then… before Dad ever got up. I was where the lake-pond thing is, and woke up in time to be doing chores, just like any other day. Eldon got in trouble because he slept too late like a lug head and missed his papers."

"How sweet Eldon!" Christine exclaimed.

"'Tis the quiet stench of early birds chewing on the poor defenseless squished worms." James whispered to give it to me. He sometimes did that sort of thing. "Don't worry Eldon. I won't hold this against you."

The girls gave James a "Don't be funny" look. This time, he ignored them.

You know, there is this thing about our town. In the early spring and summer these little shops all become like an open market, where instead of going inside you can see their products outside on carts; fish from the Greeks is no longer in refrigerated cases, but the dried fish is hung outside. Fruits, flowers, clothes, antiques, all out on the sidewalks, on carts, just so we can… ooops!! Tip them over because too many people, too many elbows, knees, shoulders. In spring, seems like the floodgates open, and every nearby town empties to our downtown.

Our conversation continued through the crowds of daytime shoppers. Christine was chattering.

"I remember a story Eldon told me about a grumpy duck that lived high in a tower. Its grumpy squawks saved the kingdom from an evil but scared dragon, who only imagined the duck to be a huge creature of immense proportions! The duck was called Duck Buddy."

"So Christine, that's why you've always called Uncle Buddy, 'Duck Buddy'!" Kasie laughed.

Kasie Dancing

We bought some smoked fish from Old Salt. One was enough for the three of us; Kasie wouldn't touch fish. We chewed on some strawberries, watched the shoppers knock over tables, drank coffee in a cafe, listened to Christine act out something she read, heard Jenkins and Fred from two tables away talking about Henderson's flying abilities, and went to an old monster movie where this cricket takes over Tokyo. It was a pretty funny movie. James and I made rude comments throughout the movie. Kasie and Christine didn't understand the idea of going to a film to make fun of it. But they humored us… somewhat. Kasie and Christine were talking about all the reasons it was good to not have a boyfriend. At the time, Christine was thinking of not going out with that boy anymore because? I don't know. I think it had to do with the fact he was teasing her a lot about the work she was doing to help the Henderson farm out. Even though he was sixteen years old, he wasn't entirely mature. It was a confusing conversation at the movie…

"Reasons why it's okay to go oh-so-lo-me-oh! Solo, no boyfriend," Kasie said. "You can eat artichoke and onion pizza and not have to worry about impressing anyone with your lovely breath."

James: "That guy looks about as smart as a Moron School drop-out."

Christine: "You can wear platforms without having to worry about being taller than shrimps!"

Me: "Actually, he's too stupid to be a moron drop out."

Kasie: "You don't have to watch movies like this one! You can see chick flicks as often as you want."

James: "Oh look! Here everybody runs! Then they stop to see if he's still chasing them, how lame can you get?!"

Christine: "Got a zit on your forehead? Who cares?"

James: "I do?" (He touched his forehead feeling for one.)

Kasie: " No more badgering your friends to find out if he REALLY likes you, and if you don't wanna wash you hair? Then don't!! Oh… and there's no need to explain why a brownie topped with chocolate ice cream, doused in peanut butter and hot fudge served with milk is a great lunch."

Me: "I think this guy's the next victim."

Christine: "That's funny Kasie!! Your Gram's cat will be a lot happier now that no one's picking it up by it's tail."

Kasie: "No more having to share half of your candy bar. You can eat both candy bars yourself! Two for me. None for you."

Me: "WHAT DO YOU MEAN YOU WON'T SHARE KASIE?! What do you got?"

Christine laughed so hard she accidentally snorted.

Kasie then said, "When something cracks you up, you can laugh and snort and not have to be embarrassed about it. You're with friends."

Kasie commenced with snorting. Loud, earth-shattering snorting. Christine timidly joined her. Then little by little she got mildly louder. It sounded more like a sneeze when Christine did it than like Kasie's foghorn. They both giggled like fiends between snorts, which only made it worse.

Kasie was the loudest snorter, but Christine just needed practice, or something. James hid his head under his hands, just like I did. Our schoolmates were in this theater after all!

In just ten days I would be leaving my friends for my trip to Washington DC. How would I do that? I mean, really?

It was early May and yet it felt like summer was just about to hit us. This was life at its finest in Apple Harbor, for us, just being kids.

* * * * *

Sometime around midnight Kasie woke me up from a deep sleep. We had spent the night at the Henderson's farm with Christine, including James.

She was dressed in jeans and a faded gray sweatshirt. I rubbed the sleep from my eyes and didn't say anything. I knew she wanted me to follow her, so I did. As we stepped outside the farmhouse, the light of the full moon hit us. The stars were brilliant, I could see every single one of them. I looked to Kasie for understanding, and realized that there was more to this than just her need to get out. She led me by the hand to the open field, where I could hear millions of crickets chirping. It was an incredibly peaceful sound.

Then I saw Christine lost in her dance, just as she had sometimes danced among the monuments of Pine Grove Cemetery. She had spent a few years as a child learning ballet. She was so graceful to watch, so free! I knew this dance was for God; she was totally unencumbered, like a deer. To see this was like watching a flower blooming before our eyes. As she raised her arms and unfolded her hands, then went into a pose called an attitude, which is where she stood on one leg, raised the other behind her, then spun herself into a frenzy. She also did a pose called the arabesque.

"I love life and I love living it for Him!" Christine yelled, as she

raised her right arm and threw her right leg back, and continued. "I am strengthened when I realize God's unlimited provision; don't we have the most amazing God?!"

I looked at Kasie and she was crying. It suddenly hit me with a force I hadn't recognized before. For Christine to lose this farm would be to lose so much and I understood that I also didn't want us to lose this either! That must not happen! Where else in all of Apple Harbor could we be ourselves, in every nook and cranny of town someone might be ready to condemn us all as crazy if she were to dance for God like this, or we were to have a water fight, or just being kids. Could we talk to the animals or be silly to our hearts content at the Hayfield Mall?

Kasie's eyes were full of tears, mine were a little wet. Both of us with utterly overwhelmed hearts joined Christine in her dance, our hands locked and our hearts felt like one. I had never done that before, broken these unwritten rules. 'Guys don't dance and guys don't cry.' But I didn't care. I had to join my sister and Christine, to see as they saw and be moved as they were moved. I too wanted to thank God for all His encouragement, for this place, for our friendship, for everything!

Although James was standing besides the wooden fence, he would not join us. He didn't get it.

"What in the world Eldon?" he asked me in a demanding tone.

"Get over it James. I'm happy. I can't explain it."

"You're getting weird. You need more guy friends. This is crazy!"

"Lord bless you, I hope you get weird too!" I answered.

"That'll never happen. Goodnight," he replied, shaking his head.

"Join us!" Christine and Kasie asked, but he ignored them. He walked away, going to bed. We danced in circles, spinning each other around and laughing, worshipping and laughing some more, until we fell at a heap in the hay. We were exhausted.

We spent the better part of an hour saying nothing, just gazing up at the heavens. Then they talked to God in their own way. We had so many things to be thankful for, and that was the gist of their prayers. I felt too much to talk or pray or anything. How I got to bed that night I'll never know.

The next morning, Sunday morning Christine was called to give the first of five such presentations to the area churches, starting with our own Sunny Valley Baptist. She was so nervous, you'd think she was going to her electrocution.

She was there a full half-hour before services started and pacing furiously.

"Do I look okay Eldon? What do you think?"

"You're fine, you'll be fine; this isn't like your playing for Carnegie Hall or something important like Yankee Stadium, and it's only your friends or a bunch of idiots. James and I will be there." I was trying to loosen her up by teasing her a bit.

"I know, I know, but… ohhhhh! I got to pray!!"

So she got behind the velvet deep red curtains of the baptistery, where an old barn door served as floor boards when various children weren't getting dunked beneath. A hunter green space rug covered the spot. There sure was a lot of junk back here. Church junk, so I guess it was okay.

For a long time she didn't say anything. Then she asked me to read her the Psalms… she had me stop after I read Psalm 56:3 "Whenever I am afraid I will trust in thee."

"Eldon, pray with me, okay? Just agree with me first."

"Agree with you? Like in a contract?"

"Just pray like you mean it Eldon. Like Kasie and I did, you know, last night?" She became shy when she said that, as if she had betrayed a secret. But then, soon enough she went on talking to the Lord as if He were her Papa. Just like last night again.

"Hello Father God… Daddy. You know I'm really scared and that I'm not able to do this. Soooooooo, please kill the butterflies in my stomach so we can get this done just the way You want. I trust You. I know You are good at your word Papa. I love You so very very much. Thanks."

I didn't know I was supposed to pray now because she never said AMEN. You're supposed to say AMEN. She didn't.

"Go ahead Eldon."

" Uh… Heavenly Father God of creation, we, uh, beseecheth thee to empower thy continence upon thy handmaiden for the service here she wants to do. AMEN."

She looked up a bit confused, but thanked me for praying with her.

"That's what agreeing in prayer means Eldon. You pray for the same thing together."

It seemed the part of the service where she got to talk never would happen. They all sang about fifteen dozen songs it seemed, with all forty verses and side notes as well. It felt like they even sang the copyright and the Latin numbers for the year it was manufactured. "MMMCMMLMNOP, oh… MMM… MCM… MNLOP."

I did tend to daydream during these songs. It was already getting hot, and the board of trustees had put off voting on a ventilation system. Mr. Wrensters said that people don't need no air conditioning, they could just open up a window. How would Christine survive that?

Although Pastor John had tried to explain the advantages of the system, he even brought in a salesman with his charts and graphs and neat diagrams… but they were never convinced. It seemed these were seriously cheap people. There were Sundays the deacons had seeded the collection plate and, as I was the boy who went around passing it I got to see allot of things most people didn't see. This particular Sunday they even used a larger bowl

"To ensure a larger return." That alone seemed to work. Because Mrs. Henderson didn't want Mrs. Markle to think just because they were farmers they couldn't give a little, I saw her give Mrs. Markle that little look where the corner of her lips would curl almost into an upside down ball and Mrs. Markle looked back, yawning, oblivious to it all. But Mrs. Henderson thought Mrs. Markle had yawned AT HER, but she hadn't. She was just tired from grading papers all weekend. So Mrs. Henderson yells out, "GIVE ME BACK THAT BOWL NOW!" And so I had to reach over a bunch of people and hand it back to her. She put in another five and gave Mrs. Markle a look of triumph, but by now Mrs. Markle had looked away because Mrs. Henderson's curled lips had made her very uneasy. It made me uneasy.

Mr. Guluzzy would throw in a twenty just because he loved the church, and had paid off his fishing boat, and Mr. Jenkins couldn't throw anything in because he threw out the brakes when Mr. Henderson had nearly killed him on Main Street with that biplane incident. He had to walk to church, but dad had picked him up when he saw him walking. It's hard to fit four people in a Volkswagen, never mind five.

Now Pastor John announced. " Today's collection goes out to the fundraiser which Christine Solanski will now announce. It's for the Henderson farm fund."

At this announcement, I saw Mrs. Henderson's jaw fall, and her face turn about as red as the tomatoes that Mrs. Gomez had won Blue Ribbons in last years County Fair.

I fully expected Christine to fall apart; I know when I once had to wait in the front of Principle Dalton's Office, that the waiting nearly drove me crazy. I had knocked out Balligrino by accident when he had kept tapping my shoulder, and in my effort to push him away I had slammed his forehead with my lock. He fell to the floor like a sack of potatoes. I didn't mean to do it. I had to wait and wait and wait. The waiting was worse than anything Mr. Dalton had said to me that day. I imagined it was just awful for poor Christine, who probably by now had found the butterflies tied up in all sorts of complicated knots in her stomach.

Anyways, back to Christine, she walked up before he congregation and stood in front of that long thin box used to hide knocking knees and shaking notes. We called it the S. D. F. S., for 'Sermon Delivery Firing System', where you probably would call it a pulpit.

She looked strangely calm, smiling as was about to speak.

"She must be in denial," I said. " She can't yet see the noose around her little neck."

"What?" James asked me, confused.

"She doesn't look nervous. She must be depressed or in denial."

"Not with that grin on her face Eldon."

Christine's voice boomed. "Hello, hello everybody. I wanted to offer you the opportunity to a day of fun at the Town Green on behalf of my uncle and aunt, the Hendersons.

"They recently lost their livestock barn and are in a lot of debt. I believe a fundraiser would be a great chance to show Christian charity, and simply have fun while doing it. My idea is if the adults who had the fair last year would sponsor the events we could do what is said every year at the fair… have the fair twice. You know how at the end of the fair every year mayor gives a speech bemoaning the fact we don't have two fairs? Well, I always hear crowds agree. We could have the same events… pie eating contests, cookie sales, sack races, music from some local bands and maybe more. There's a lot of talent here in Apple Harbor and throughout the county. I hope you'll agree and take part in signing up. You have soo much to offer. I will be playing violin myself, you'll see my name on the list of volunteers. The mayor suggested the dates from June 12th to June 19th; of course it has to be decided at the town meeting if the churches can use the Town Green. Thank you very much!"

Everyone who knew Christine couldn't believe their eyes. Here she was presenting the plan with great ease in front of nearly a hundred people. Next week she'd present the idea to four other churches, the morning service to the Lutherans, the evening service to the Catholics, the Wednesday night service at the Presbyterians, and the Friday night youth meeting at Open Bible Assembly. I guess if the Lord could part the Red Sea, He had no problem giving Christine the confidence she'd need to do this.

Mrs. Wallstien asked Pastor John for her money back as people were shaking his hand on their way out. He just laughed and said, "You think this is some kind of department store? Got your receipt?"

Mrs. Wallstien didn't smile back.

— chapter 9 —

Illegally Parked!

"What's going on out there? Why that Smhidt has ALL of the traffic blocked, he's parked in the middle of the street!" Jenkins yelled from the Tinti's banquet room

"Helen is illegally parked Jenkins?"

"I AM NOT! WHY… why can't you be quiet Jenkins?"

"No. It's her son Jason. That guy's a fish at the bars."

"He's not that bad."

Fred was trying to smooth things over a little. He didn't mind giving Helen a hard time, but didn't want Jenkins to hurt the woman like this. As I said before, Jenkins was always just like that, loud, unthinking. That was just his way. If Fred saw an opening to lightly tease a buddy or the ladies at Tinti's or Old Salt's, he'd take it. But he knew when to shut up. If you ever said " Hi" to Fred, he would pretty soon consider you fair game. He was a quiet talker, light on the teasing. He gave Jenkins the hardest time because of his mouth, which seemed to run on empty if you know what I mean.

" Helen, your son does great construction work," Fred said.

" Thank you."

As we looked out the window we saw Officer Solanski lead Jason out to his squad car, in cuffs. About five minutes later Tinti's got a call and Babbs asked me to move the truck.

"I'm not legal for on the road vehicles, only tractors," I tried to explain.

"Just park it behind the florist shop a block away Eldon."

As I walked out Babbs yelled. “The dispatcher says the keys are in the ignition. He leaves some cookies in the glove compartment if you’re hungry.”

“Boy, you leave them alone!”

“Helen, Jason asked for the boy to move his truck. He was the one making the offer.”

“I’m not hungry Mrs. Smhidt, honest,” I said, taking my cue from Fred’s look. Why make a bad situation worse, right?

While I was moving the Smhidt construction truck, Jason Smhidt was being hauled off to appear immediately before Judge Parker, no questions asked. It seemed Jason had piled up a great number of these parking violations, and had merely torn up the tickets for years. No one ever expected Judge Parker to ever issue a warrant for his arrest.

But this was a different kind of arrest. As I said, he was hauled off to the judge’s office immediately.

“What in the… I want an explanation NOW Parker!”

“You get your rights read Smhidt? He treated you nice now, didn’t he?”

“Well, yeah, but you can’t go hauling people off like that!”

“Let me explain something to you Smhidt. What we’re having here is an off the record conversation, a conference if you please. You get my drift?”

“Well, I just don’t like being dragged in like this.”

“Would you prefer the accommodations downtown?”

“On what charges?”

“Besides the parking violations you mean? Well, the district attorney’s office has fielded a host of complaints from some of your customers of overcharging.”

“That’s a lie and you know it!”

“I have the reports here. You charged Mrs. McDogal for twice the lumber you really used. I guess you didn’t realize her husband did the orders at the lumber yard?”

Jason Smhidt turned white. His confidence evaporated to nothing.

Judge Parker gave a soft answer. "I'm willing to make a certain arrangement if you'd be pleased to listen."

"Yes sir?" Smhidt's voice had also softened considerably.

"The McDogals won't bring up any charges if you and your boys build them a deck in their backyard. That would equal the wood you overcharged."

"I can do that."

"There's one more thing. This will cost you and you're under no obligation you understand to comply. But I was reading in the *Apple Harbor Gazette* about a young lady who has been trying to raise funds for the Henderson's barn. I want you to make a sizable donation to her efforts."

"How sizable?"

"An anonymous party is donating the lumber and what-not. You simply provide the labor. You're under no obligation but I think you should know something."

"Yes?"

"You heard about that balloonist whose life Solanski here saved from that trigger happy Bacote in Hayford County?"

"Well, yeah, I did I guess..."

"He would have drowned before those bucket heads realized it. That... was my brother. He is very grateful to Officer Solanski so he'd appreciate any help you'd offer to his daughter's fundraising efforts."

"Why should I do that?"

"Besides the fear of a summer in jail?"

"Yeah?"

"He is the fellow who audits businesses when these sort of complaints are made, and he'd really appreciate your help if you catch my drift."

"No obligation huh?" Smhidt scoffed. "You mean he works for..."

"Yeah. S.N.P."

"I'll be happy to donate my services then."

"I have your word?"

"Believe me, you do Judge Parker, sir."

"We have an understanding then. You're free to go."

At this point Dorothy barged into the office.

"I'm sorry, but there's been a disturbance at your house Frank! Seems some kids spray painted graffiti all over your place. They have one boy in custody already."

"Who?! What?!"

"'Polack', some swear words, ' Jesus freak' that kind of thing. It was your daughter's boyfriend."

"James? Eldon? That's impossible!"

"Your daughter's BOYFRIEND. Not her friends."

"My daughter has a boyfriend?"

Dorothy shook her head and mumbled, "Figures."

Judge Parker said, "You better take the afternoon off Frank. I'd ask the Chief if I were you."

"He already has that permission Judge Parker. He's off whether he likes it or not as a matter of fact," Dorothy yelled.

"This puts me in a pickle," Solanski said to Judge Parker.

"Why?"

"I'm filling in tomorrow for Darby, the youth offender officer. That'll be a real conflict of interest if I have to see that kid in my office."

" If you don't press charges you won't have to see him in Darby's office."

"Like that's going to happen. Of course I'm going to press charges."

"I have to suggest you don't if you want retribution. I can see that he repairs the place and gets whatever help he needs."

"You mean a psych doctor?"

"Why don't you look at the damages and decide what you want to do tomorrow. The kid will be held at the Youth Detention Center in Hayford for 48 hours, until formal charges are brought on him… or dropped."

As he walked out Mr. Solanski muttered, "I probably better talk to Christine about this boy."

Dorothy yelled, " He wanted to be caught you know."

"Why do you say that?"

"He was found sitting on your front porch with the spray can in his hand."

* * * * *

"Hello John, thanks for seeing me here."

"Well, that's fine, I heard the news and was pretty surprised myself," Pastor John said.

"I'm not sure what to do with this one. Frankly, after seeing the damages I wanted to… it scared me how enraged I felt. Especially after I saw how it affected Christine. She seemed pretty upset."

"Craig is a good boy. I don't understand this Frank."

"More coffee boys?" Babbs asked them.

"Sure Babbs. Thanks."

"You Frank?"

"No thank you Babbs. Excuse us please? This is a very private conversation."

"Sorry Frank, Pastor Axworthy."

" I'm not a religious guy John. I transferred to Apple Harbor because I figured it'd be safer for Emma; my wife was expecting Christine then… my work was following me if you follow me. I knew this town's biggest problems were occasionally the DWI or a fight now and then, and I'd rather deal with that then what I saw in the cities around Hayford. Finally we moved here when Christine was just about four years old."

"I see a lot too Frank, really."

"I'm just saying that's why you don't see me in church."

"Hmm? I don't follow you."

"I know the congregation too well. Unfortunately. Even here in Apple Harbor."

"Oh, that. Yeah, I hear more than you think Frank. I'm not in some ivory tower above all this. I hear the sorrows of adultery, I know how it has torn families apart, I know grown men who have wept over the mistakes of their infidelities, drunkenness, their problems with anger, their every weakness. The Ten Commandments were written to show us how very weak we all are. However, I also have seen redemption's work in many cases and I see so much good. "

"How do you figure that?"

"I won't give you a case by case story, but I have known parishioners who have learned the power of forgiveness, the glory of grace right in the middle of the muck of their humanity. Being human is not always a pretty picture. But God works to redeem humanity."

"Listen, what should I do about Craig? Your opinion?"

"Have you prayed about it?"

"I'm not a religious man John. I just know you're known around town for being good with the teens."

"I didn't ask you if you were religious Frank. I asked you if you prayed about this."

"No. I wouldn't know what to say. I'm agnostic. I only took Christine to church because, well, my wife thought it was a good idea if she got religious education, as it helped Emma cope with her problems. Thought it couldn't hurt."

"Would it bother you if I prayed for you and this situation?"

"Just don't do that here, now, okay?"

"All right. I won't. I respect that Frank. But I think you should have him repair the damages. Either way you'd have to face him, now wouldn't you?"

"I don't like this. I don't want him around my wife or daughter. I don't trust him."

"Have you talked to him?"

"Not yet."

"You want me to do that, and get back to you?" Pastor John asked Frank.

"I guess I do, guess that's why I'm here."

"It might help you figure out why he did it."

"I don't really care WHY he did it," Frank said. "Just want to know if he's dangerous."

"Frank, he never before even had a misdemeanor against him, did he?"

"No. So?"

"Then I think I should talk to him. I know the boy and..."

"Spare me the speech about all people being really good at heart."

"Actually I would never say that about people Frank."

"All right. Talk to him. Then I'll decide, OK?"

"Thank you. I'll get back to you tomorrow."

The next afternoon Pastor John was waiting at Officer Solanski's home, and Christine and her mother were sitting in the living room. I came over having heard the news at school. When I rang the doorbell Pastor John answered the door.

"Hi Eldon, maybe you better come by later, okay?"

"I know I should, but I thought..."

Mrs. Solanski saw me and said, "It's all right John, the Coopers are probably the best thing right now for my daughter."

I said, "I just figured a walk would do her good, she wasn't at school and, well..."

Christine popped her head from behind her mom, saying, "Oh, hi Eldon, where's Kasie? James?"

"Kasie is at the farm with James. I just thought a walk would be more fun for you than being home right now."

"As a matter of fact it would!"

We walked in silence under the gray skies. But after a while I noticed Christine was whistling.

"What's that?"

" Canon in D by Taco Bell."

"I never knew it!"

"Really? You must eat out more."

"Yeah, I'm starving now as a matter of fact. You know what though? I don't think much of Craig's art."

"Me either. He isn't much of an expressionist nor does he capture the... the..." Christine couldn't think of the art words, so I broke in.

"The essence of a true cubist. I don't think his brush strokes conveyed the depth of..."

"His depravity? His pain, his anguish?" Christine asked.

"Yeah." I answered simply.

Christine was laughing again. It was really good to hear.

"Where will you run away too then Christine?"

"I haven't decided Eldon, how about you?" she said grinning from ear to ear.

"I decided I'm going to move with my dog to Australia. I looked in an encyclopedia and noticed that the ACME Travel agency claims Australia doesn't have any problems this time of year. It's really very nice when you think about it."

"Eldon, there's only one thing."

"Uh, yeah?"

"You don't have a dog."

"Okay. I'll bring the dogs I take when I roller-skate on my route then. Or most likely bring Bear."

"Sounds like you got it all figured out."

"You going to school tomorrow?" I asked.

"I wanted to go to school TODAY. Dad wouldn't hear it. I think he imagines me as some sort of porcelain doll that needs protection. Really, I'm not going to get cracked over this. It'll take a lot more than that to get me to the loony bin." Then she looked at me, grinned and said, "Well, Kasie or you will probably get me there someday."

"HEY!!"

"Want half of a Nut Bar?" she asked me. "Sure. Thanks. Can I have the other half too?"

"No Eldon," she said laughing. "I think NOT. I think I'll just move to Alaska."

"Alaska? I'll ask her," I said. Christine rolled her eyes and smirked as I continued, "Kasie might like that. You know Christine if bad news really bothers you maybe you could find some way to take a mini vacation from it, read comics, watch a cartoon or do something you especially like doing."

"Oh, don't worry about that. My Bible, my violin all that is my vacation, and acting and I won't quit it and this isn't bothering me anymore Eldon."

"It's really not?" I asked that because I knew her. I suspected sometimes she would be brave for our benefit.

"Okay, maybe a little bit Eldon, it's just I'm tired of it being sheltered sometimes."

"You know God can even carry your prayers for everybody else when you are too tired to pray. You just throw up a quick 'Help Lord, maintain them pleeeease... would you help my friends' and He sends a maintenance angel to repair the mess they made while God restores you."

"Maintenance angel huh? I like that thought," Christine admitted.

"Were you scared or angry when you first saw it?"

"Both. I felt violated by Craig. But I know why he did it."

"Really? You must be some kind of Sherlock Holmes then, huh?" I suggested.

"Not really. He was trying for the past couple of weeks to get me to drop this whole thing with the Hendersons. He was catching a lot of grief for it from kids, even a few teachers made jokes about it."

"I heard a few comments Christine but I never figured he'd pull that. It's rather drastic don't you think?"

"Now he'll be popular. He never really was my boyfriend like he thought he was anyhow. I just saw him as someone to hang with. He just sat on our front door and told the police he was my boyfriend. WHATEVER."

"How can you be smiling as if we're talking about someone else? How can you cope with this like it's nothing?"

"I first take my tears to God, then to my mom. If I think Mom can't handle it, I ask Him about that too Eldon. It's really not my problem anymore. I know I'll be okay."

"But it did bother you?"

"Yes. I thought we covered this. Are you a shrink? You are kind of short."

"Now it doesn't bother you, and no I'm taller than you by two inches. Okay. I guess you took your Australian vacation then. The good Lord sent you clear to the other side of the world. That's cool Christine."

"He covers me in His love and care."

When we finally got back to her house, her father and Pastor John were discussing what Craig had confessed to Pastor John. We heard the tail end of that, and her father was considering this when Christine announced to him:

"If you had asked me Father, but you didn't, I could have told you that. He just wants to be popular and not be seen with the Jesus girl. I suggest you just make him repaint the outside of the house when Mom's home, and please drop the matter entirely."

She hugged and then kissed her father on the cheek. " I do love you Daddy, but you can be so annoying sometimes. Now can I go to school?"

"Uh, yeah, okay. Yeah. Yeah to both. But he can paint the house only when I'm home though."

"We're through if that's what you're worried about. He won't hurt us or anything Daddy, really."

"I'm glad to hear that but it's simply a precaution honey, okay?"

She looked at him for a moment, sizing up his words and answered. "Okay Daddy. By the way, you should really come to church next week. I'll play violin, Cassandra, Veronica and I are part of a string quartet. It'll be fun. You might learn something."

"That sounds safe enough I guess. When does the quartet start?"

"Daddddddy! You got to come to the WHOLE service okay?"

She was playfully pulling at his sleeve. He smiled at her and said, "Maybe, I just don't know. I'm allergic to pews."

I turned to leave figuring this was a private family conversation, and just before I got completely out the door I heard Christine say, "Hey Eldon, thanks for the Australian cruise… it was sooo much fun!"

"Huh… oh, yeah… sure."

"Thanks for stopping by Eldon. Take some cheesecake with you." Mrs. Solanski handed me a plate of it covered in plastic wrap.

Early the next morning I was going to walk with Yellow Bear, whom Mr. Henderson dropped off. He had the pick-up and several cans of paint, brushes and a ladder in the back.

"Thanks Eldon. I appreciate this on such short notice!"

"It's no problem. About half the dogs won't be walked now until

I get back from DC. The owners feel a little more comfortable with someone they know."

"That'll be good for Christine then. How many dogs will she be walking?"

"Three or Four. Rowsers, Bear, Lass and maybe one more."

"Well Eldon, I have to get going. I have some work to do."

He drove off, and I got to Christine's house to drop off their paper. I rang the bell and Mrs. Solanski answered the door.

"Christine's not up to going on the route with you today. She said maybe tomorrow."

"She sick?"

"Yes, so she needs a little more time. She'll see you and Kasie at school today later; I'll drive her myself. Under my condition I can't be around wet paint too long."

Mrs. Solanski was expecting a baby in six months.

As I was leaving Mr. Henderson came out of the backyard, with the ladder. Jenkins and Old Salt were there as well, holding paint cans and plastic wrap. I also saw Fred with another ladder.

"Is it almost warm enough to paint yet?" Jenkins asked

"Very close. Five minutes ought to do it," Mr. Henderson replied.

"Well, we're sure here early then." Jenkins grumbled.

"Mr. Henderson, do you know how to play hooky from a correspondence school?" James asked him.

"That's a groaner coming." Mr. Jenkins sighed.

"Just mail them an empty envelope! AAAAH!"

Fred laughed, but Jenkins just glared at him.

" Now Ralph Jenkins, don't discourage the boy."

"Whatever Mr. Fred Murphy… I'd rather not encourage him."

" Boy, one thing I've learned about being a clock watcher…"

"Yes Mr. Henderson?" James asked.

"A clock passes time by keeping its hands busy." Old Salt said, finishing the joke.

I forgot about my paper route having grabbed a ladder to steady Old Salt. Several of the immediate neighbors and church members were bringing treats to Mrs. Solanski.

As time went on more and more people showed up. Fred brought us some stir sticks, Randy Nelson got two more cans of paint that he donated from the hardware store, Babbs brought the guys some coffee on her way to her work at Tinti's, Doctor Anderson stopped by just to chat and wound up painting a good part of the porch and Pastor John dropped a can of paint on his head when he had also just stopped having seen a crowd growing. Nothing like yellow streaks of paint on a black jogging suit. He looked like a bee. Fortunately there was a hose nearby for such disasters. Uncle Buddy stopped by briefly when he saw Pastor John wiping the paint off his face with an old towel.

"I was wondering when I'll get paid for helping with the bell?"

"Come to the church tomorrow, I'll be at the office then. "

I was surprised at his patience with my uncle, considering how much paint he had in his eyes, face and jogging suit.

Several of the immediate neighbors and church members were bringing treats to Mrs. Solanski. Within an hour the painting was finished, within another hour and ten minutes no one knew we were there. Yeah, I was late for school that day.

When Craig's father showed up that afternoon with Craig to start the painting, of course they were surprised to see everything completed. Christine led them into the dining room and prepared them a small treat. Her mother was downstairs doing laundry. Christine brought Mr. Roman some cheese and crackers on a plate, along with some punch.

"My son is supposed to do retribution," Mr. Roman said. "But everything's done."

"It's my guess Dad will ask him to clean the garage out."

" Piece of cake," Craig mumbled to himself.

"You haven't seen our garage," Christine said it matter-of-factly.

"Get started. I mean now," Mr. Roman ordered.

"Shouldn't we wait until her father decides?" Craig asked.

"Mrs. Solanski..." Mr. Roman saw her carrying a basket up the stairs. "Do you think it would be all right if my boy cleans up your garage?"

"You better figure on doing something else. Frank never gets rid of anything."

"This is really good cheese," then added. "Oh? When are you due Mrs. Solanski?" Mr. Roman commented seeing her growing form.

"I'm due in October, but if Christine had it her way the baby would wait till her birthday in late November," Mrs. Solanski said good-naturedly.

Mr. Roman's anger flared up as his son. "You crazy boy to treat these good people like this? You know her father is a respected police officer in town. Why you do that?"

Christine was under the impression Craig had heard this conversation before, but that he was sorry too. She couldn't decide if he was sorry he had been caught or truly feeling bad about what he had done. He wouldn't look anyone in the eye. His expression revealed absolutely nothing.

"She's a nice girl. You should not have done this."

"I... I'm going to rake the leaves." Craig got up and left for the yard.

"We don't have any leaves, Craig! Craig! None that need..." Christine couldn't finish; he was already out the door. " No leaves..." She started to laugh.

"He's a good boy, my son. In the choir and never make trouble before. A good Christian boy. I do not understand this."

"It's okay Mr. Roman. I understand." Christine put her hand on his shoulder and smiled as she handed him another glass of punch from the pitcher. "This doesn't change my opinion of your family. I know you love the Lord. I know Craig does too."

"I'm just sorry Mrs. Solanski, Christine."

The large Italian man looked imposing, his shoulders and well-defined arms showed his many years of labor in construction. His wavy dark black hair was long enough to look good without being shabby. He pleaded at them with those big sad eyes, and Christine had to lose his gaze. She saw too much of her friend Craig in those eyes, in his expression and sorrow.

– chapter 10 –

Mrs. Hoppenhetter Breaks Forth

That very morning Mrs. Hophenetter, who was known as a recluse went out on her porch for the very first time in years. She hadn't stepped out in so very long, never saw a reason for it. She had enough money to hire neighborhood boys to rake her yard or run out for her groceries; Pastor John would call on her and she'd give him a list of errands. She had her books, her radio, her plants and several cats and that miniature poodle. She kept herself busy and never bothered with anyone. But this morning she wrapped herself in her heaviest coat, a scarf and thick leather gloves. She looked herself over in the closet mirror and grinned.

"Audrey Hepburn, eat your heart out," she bragged, as she tossed a scarf over her head. It was bright red, the only color on her.

As she walked to Tinti's the Nelson twins gave her a funny look, this being May and already quiet warm by 9 AM. But how would she know? Tracy Anson, who was only four years old saw the shoebox in Mrs. Hophenetters arm and asked her about it. She gave the curly haired little girl a quick look over and saw the question was genuine. This wasn't a child looking to mock her.

"It's a time machine honey. It has pictures of our past in here."

The child smiled at her. That was enough to know. She turned around and waved, saying, "Have a nice day lady, bye bye."

Mrs. Hophenetter felt encouraged. She walked into Tinti's and the bells announced her arrival. Fred and Jenkins looked up from their breakfast. She noticed they had pastel yellow splotches of paint all over their clothes and hair. To her right were several of the blacks, the basketball players with my friend Bo among them. They smiled at her, she returned a shy grin. She looked over to her left, and saw Helen and several women whispering and pointing at her.

"The midnight gardener." Helen grumbled, pointing at her.

Mrs. Hophenetter decided to take a booth closest to the counter where Fred and Jenkins sat. The sign said "Suit Yourself" but was supposed to read "Seat Yourself". Some smart aleck changed the chalk walk in sign. Which was comfortably far away from those meddling quitters, and gave her room for her pictures. She spread the pictures out in front of her. Here were pictures of a much younger Anderson, Nelson and so many of the local boys. There were pictures of nurses and local girls stationed in England just before the invasion. They were singers with the WAF. No wonder they called her Tim a shutterbug. How many years had it been since she really looked at these pictures?

"How are you Mrs. Hophenetter?" Bo asked her.

"You are sweet to ask me Bo. Do you still paint young man?"

"Yeah, I love art. You should stop by our church sometime; Mom says she'd love to see you there. Last week's sermon was 'We're Not Victims Anymore!'"

"You sure no one would mind?" Mrs. Hophenetter asked.

"Because you're white? No, we have all colors at Mount Zion," Bo said, then apologized as if he had said something wrong.

"I meant because I'm old. I might be dangerous. I'm the crazy woman." Mrs. Hophenetter shot a look at Helen, who turned her gaze away embarrassed.

"What's that got to do with anything? Mom was always asking about you, she liked your style. She said you were hard on us kids and all. You gave us a lot of... grief. We were used to your craziness a long time ago."

The other boys looked at her and laughed. It was a friendly laugh.

Howard, our school's tallest basketball player, looked right at Helen and said loud enough for everyone to hear, "You know, she might be a 'Midnight Gardener', but I hear you got other habits Mrs. Smhidt. Like running your mouth off too much."

Fred and Jenkins both said, "Amen!" to that, which abruptly stopped any reaction from her part, or the other ladies.

Bo gave Howard a look, which said, in effect, "Don't say anymore."

Mrs. Hophenetter smiled. "I'll be happy to go to your church. You say 'Hi' to your mother for me, now, okay?"

"I'll do that," Bo answered.

Howard joked with Mrs. H. "We'd like to see you there, we need more crazy people you know. I mean nice crazy people."

Mrs. Hophenetter laughed joyfully, saying, " You boys are crazy enough! Your preacher is it still Frankie Gramm?"

" Yeah. That's him," Bo answered.

Mrs. Hophenetter pulled out a picture of Frankie from among the many in her piles. It was a photo of a young black gunner, looking happy and far too young in a uniform, which was a size too large for him. Standing next to him were Tim Hophenetter and Sgt. Smhidt sitting in a jeep, all three laughing at a private joke.

"That can't be Pastor Gramm, really?!" Bo exclaimed.

"Oh, yeah, he was a much skinnier man then. But that was over thirty-five years ago. We all change a little at a time Bo."

"I'm never getting that big. He sure let those potlucks stick to him! But you'll see, I'm staying skinny and fine looking! The ladies will always fight over this brother!" Bo said, handing the picture to Howard, and it made the rounds back to Mrs. Hophenetter.

"It's not a crime to be heavy." Mrs. Hophenetter smiled. " But I've always been underweight myself, a bean pole."

The boys got up from the booth, leaving money for the bill. Howard was dribbling a basketball without even thinking about it. It was second nature to him. Mrs. Doglas asked him to stop. " Please…" sounding as patient as she could, you could sense the fear in her voice. Helen wouldn't even look his way. He apologized and stopped. They left with goodbyes to Mrs. Hophenetter, Fred and Jenkins.

Fred looked at Mrs. Hophenetter and smiled.

"It's good to see you again," he told her.

"Thank you Fred. It's good to be back."

Jenkins said, "You did a good job on that place of yours."

"Well Jenkins, I might be doing some remodeling. I want to open up the yard a bit."

"Really? You think you'll need some help?" Fred asked.

"I'm not a charity case, I pay. I pay for everything," Mrs. Hophenetter answered.

"We understood that," Jenkins replied in a kind voice.

"Well, okay then. You got any large panels of Plexiglas? Something we could use in a fence?" Mrs. Hophenetter asked them.

"I'm sure Nelson's Hardware could special order something for us," Fred said. " But you'll have to give us more details."

"I'd like your help," Mrs. Hophenetter said. " And that SON OF YOURS HELEN!"

Fred and Jenkins laughed again.

"This sounds interesting," Jenkins said. "Right up our alley. After hours."

"Yeah, maybe around the night shift!"

The three all shared a laugh.

"I'll tell you more later, just stop by after work sometime. You know the place," Mrs. Hophenetter says.

Babbs finally stopped by Mrs. Hophenetter's table. It wasn't that busy, but her boss had her painting the banquet room pipes all these bright colors. He expected it to be a dead morning. It wasn't quiet that slow. Just like Fred and Jenkins she had splotches of paint all over her.

"What in the world?! Is everyone crazier than me today?" Mrs. Hophenetter asked, marveling at the sight of Babbs with paint splotches in her hair, clothes and fingers.

" What you got there hon?" Babbs asked Mrs. Hophenetter. She saw that Mrs. Hophenetter had the pictures spread out over the whole counter, with no room for the black coffee she drinks. When was the last time Mrs. H. had been here?

"Babbs, you'll find this most interesting. Kasie Cooper found this shoebox upstairs in my attic and it's loaded with pictures of the veterans of Apple Harbor. I haven't ever looked at them until she brought them down."

Babbs took a seat right next to her, ignoring Bossman's call of "ORDER UP!"

"I have to wash up first you know Mr. Jackie Hammil!!" Babbs yelled.

She flipped through and was very surprised to see the excellent condition the photographs were in. She recognized Fred and Jenkins, Bossman, Henri Nelson, Doctor Anderson and a much younger Judge Parker. What a find! These pictures showed the life of these friends before the war in their everyday common life, at the barbershop, walking in the Green with their girls, Christmas parties, dances and the prom of the youngest vets Fred and Jenkins. She also had pictures of bombed out buildings in France and Germany, and shell-shocked men who bore little resemblance to the boys of these Apple Harbor scenes. Even though the faces all shown half smiles, the eyes of one and all showed a great weariness.

"ORDER UP BABBS!" 'Bossman', Jackie Hammil yelled again.

"There's also this book. Notes my husband kept after the war. It was about what happened to these boys of the Black Panther Squadron."

"My husband never talks about it." Babbs sighed.

"Guess that's the difference between a real vet and a liar; oh, here's a photograph of your Darby. I'll get it copied for you if you'd like."

"He looks good in a uniform there with his friends! There's Rick Klanko and Arnie Roman, Craig's uncle! It really takes me back. Maybe you could copy some more pictures for me? I'd gladly pay you."

"BABBS! Get over here NOW!" Bossman yelled.

Babbs hurried over and placed the order before Helen and the ladies. As she did Tom Bartlet, the printer sat down opposite Mrs. Hophenetter. He looked and saw no room for coffee. He smiled anyways.

"What'cha got for me?" Tom asked.

The bells announced yet another visitor. It was a reporter from the *Apple Harbor Gazette*. She was an older woman, in her fifties, with short wavy hair and lean built and walked in a very serious manner.

"We're over here." Helen motioned to the reporter.

Fred and Jenkins left a tip, smiled at Mrs. Hophenetter then left Tinti's.

The lady reporter ignored Helen and sat down next to Tom. For the next several hours the three sat there talking, looking over the pictures and the book, and who knows what else. It got Helen and her friends terribly curious. She wanted to ask Babbs what it was about but knew that woman never told tales on anyone. And now… her eggs were cold.

And there was paint on the plate too!

— chapter 11 —

Sailing

Old Salt had a small yacht, simply called the "Grey Goose"; it was little bigger than a daysailer really except it had a toilet and cabin. He had made arrangements with our parents for Christine, Kasie and I to sail that Saturday. James wasn't interested. Saturday came pretty quickly and afterwards our parents would meet us at the Firehouse backyard for Hobo Stew with "Chief Smoky" Franks.

We were all out there at the harbor, the "Grey Goose" set for the trip with the latest in navigation and hardware. The sails, rigging and gear looked to me to be top notch. As Christine was boarding and her father waved her off, we left the harbor with the small engine taking us safely out until the mainsail could be released.

"If these waters get too choppy Eldon, you shut the engine off to prevent failure."

"Yes sir. I checked the condition of the sails at their stress points and…"

" I did that too Eldon, thanks, are your life jackets tight?" He asked us all.

We all checked, double-checked and answered, "Yes."

He told us a little about a trip up the Hudson River he took last autumn. He said, "You know, that's a hard one to take in autumn. At least for sailing. It's cold and rainy and the water's hard to navigate."

He released the mainsail once we were in open waters and told me to kill the engine. I did. The morning sun was starting to warm things up. It's always a bit cooler out sailing. I was glad for bringing my sweatshirt.

Old Salt continued. "I like this better. We have a nice south wind today. 'Though boisterous winds and Neptune's waves have toss me too and fro, by God's decree you plainly see I am Harbour'd here below.' That I read on the stone of Mariner James Barnerd in the Hudson Valley. He died in 1768."

It was too beautiful out to be haunted by those thoughts, and he wasn't trying to spread gloom, just tell us a story.

"I sailed past the George Washington Bridge at night, past the beautiful side of New York City's lights, and up to Tarrytown. I saw that big old full moon be captured by Minewawa; she crumbles it up into the stars every month. It's really worth seeing you know."

I didn't know what he was talking about. Christine's eyes lit up as if she understood and said, "I always liked that story of Minewawa."

He moved on to the present situation.

"Kasie, check the radio in the cabin for weather conditions east of here."

"Aye aye Captain!"

Like riding on glass, the yacht rode us smoothly over the Sound with the peaceful fullness of her sails arched up, and out. Clouds had been banished and swept clean for our journey. The salt smelled good as the breeze pulled up the aroma from the froth. Gulls dived and clamored overhead ever now and then. But we weren't a fishing scow.

So they'd leave with sharp wonderful shrieks and the silence of their slow moving wings, until they were free of this moving island. Such silence. I never had imagined their could be such a beautiful unearthly silence as this, broken only occasionally by a wave or the flapping of the smaller sails. None of us talked much. Not even Kasie, who was now seated besides Christine at the stern.

"Do you know what the hobbies of the sailors were in old days children?"

We didn't.

"They'd make ship models in a bottle, they'd engrave on bottles with nails, they carved wooden boxes for their ladies and made ropes."

"I know the food they had Old Salt," I said. "On the extra long voyages the sailing ships carried livestock for fresh food. Chickens and pigs, and they had dried fish and ship biscuits."

"Look through these binoculars and see if you can name the vessels out there?" Old Salt asked me.

I couldn't name but a few yachts and a tugboat or two. Kasie just called them all boats and Christine couldn't tell us anymore than I did. But that Old Salt... he recognized warships, fire control boats, and some pipe layers, an icebreaker heading for New York for supplies, and spotted two subs out resurfacing. He also pointed out some cruise ships and various large yachts.

He played the deck winch out, releasing the crank a bit. He glanced over at the mast track slides and pointed out to me the different parts of the mast.

"That's the masthead, stern stay, shroud lug, forestay, shroud spreader and those are reef hooks..." He named about fifteen things they did and how they worked, then asked us all. "Got it?"

I didn't. I couldn't remember the various names for these things, what they were used for or why; all I could do was steer the wheel (which he called a helm but most sailors called a wheel). Kasie smiled politely, not wanting to sound stupid. Christine was looking out at the waves, then pulled out a small notebook from her daypack and started writing something.

"Well," Old Salt smiled seeing the doubt in my face. "We're going large today, sailing with a fair wind abaft the beam on the portside. You see those sails? Those are my two foresails. This keeps us maintain handling in all weather conditions. Can you name some of the signal code flags?"

He showed me an unmarked page of flags. I remembered one of them.

"I have a diver down, stay clear away."

"At slow speed, yes. This one means 'I'm altering my course to starboard and that to port.' There are different flags for different ships..." Old Salt smiled, and pulled out a piece of medal object which formed an arc. "Know what this is?"

"Don't have a clue."

"Before radar and radio was invented, this was used for navigation by my grandfather, and his father before him. It's called an octant. I use a sextant at sea on the fishing voyages in the North Atlantic, and of course that's an astronomical instrument. It can be used without a stand. I also use the Decca sea charts with the radio; our receiver has the lanes of our route."

Old Salt stopped talking, having been distracted by Kasie, who was reading loudly from a paper Christine had handed her…

Where do sky and sea meet?
Out where gray sands blend with breaking waves,
I toss a polished stone into waters
That bounces forever against the tide

When murky skies give way to sudden moon
I may sail on a northeastern, but
Will the moon too be swallowed whole?
By that ever hungry sea?
I saw her consume the sun in a fiery gulp
That set the skies ablaze in crimson.
Shall I find the globes of fury and light
Surround now my silent shy ship?
Like fireflies in June?
Will comets dazzle beneath my stern
Flowing alongside the dolphins tails

Perhaps I can plunder sky's treasures
Provide for merchants those stars in this sea
Emeralds of rubies, topaz, a moon or two,
And I can cast nets for Rose Nebula
To give to my Love

Or maybe I'll just leave the sea be.
This place, where sea and sky mist together.

We were very impressed and all said so. Kasie explained that Christine wrote it, not herself.

I started to think about something that had just happened at school to Christine years before. She once came to class carrying a Bible big enough to choke a mule on when she was six years old. It was for show and tell. Of course she wouldn't get up herself to present it, which would be my job. Kids thought that was strange. In those days she'd wear clothes that were so old fashioned, and even some six year olds could be cruel about that. Yet the thing that really sticks out in my mind was her sweetness even then. Some kids called her the "Jesus girl" in reference to her faith. She could make them feel guilty just getting close to them. Especially after they had just been joking about her. Pretty soon kids just avoided her altogether, because nobody liked to feel guilty for having a little fun. Most of my friends stopped calling her those names after two years because by then she was Kasie's friend, and Kasie wouldn't put up with it. One of the girls bragged she could beat Kasie up with both arms tied behind her back, but it turned out not to be true.

The fact is Christine had been our friend since she had moved down the street at age four. It was like breathing and eating and everything else, it just came naturally. But four years later, as a young boy of nine years old I didn't completely understand the gift of her friendship. I figured since Craig Shumacker gave me a Mooser Malt candy bar, that he was my friend. He made stupid remarks about Christine, but I figured I should just forgive him, and even helped him along by contributing my own stupidity, my own remarks. And one day Christine overheard my remarks about her Bible, and she was stopped cold. Her mouth opened wide and her eyes almost watered. But the tears wouldn't come. Her shyness wouldn't allow it. I felt like the devil himself had taken a hold of my cold stony heart and twisted it into a dark place, filling me with laments. I felt as if I had done a terrible horrible thing. Which I did. Like I said, eight-year-old Christine gave me a stunned look. It was too late. I couldn't take the words back. I never said anything that stupid again, at least about her. I learned to defend a friend, and I learned about forgiveness.

Over the years a certain innocence never changed. Now, at fourteen years old, she was like a real sweet child, she would look at you and it felt like she could see into your soul. My youngest cousin did that too, but she was only six. Most people, by the time they are ten find eye contact uncomfortable for prolonged periods with anyone outside a certain circle of very close friends. But she was comfortable in her skin in spite of her shyness. She was also very happy. What a smile she had!! I had never really taken the time to notice that before, or anything else about Christine for that matter. There were too many other girls that I noticed, once I noticed girls I mean. It wasn't the smiles I noticed either.

Still, Christine did have her share of noticers. Just that week, Bobby, a son of that social worker Sue Doglas asked her out, but she wasn't interested. So he tried the "I'm lost and need someone to talk to approach." But it didn't work as he had planned. She set up a lunch appointment for him with herself, her pastor, and myself. Opps. (He declined the offer.)

He was doing all this talking right in front of Margaret, his girlfriend of the week. I was going to warn Christine. She could be so naive. Bobby started wearing that Jesus T-shirt because he wanted to mock her so much. She told him he should not wear the shirt if he's going to swear so much as kids would get confused, but she'd pray for him to stop swearing. She smiled real sweetly and said, "I'm sure you don't want to do that."

I felt like screaming, "Wake up Christine!!" right about then. Swearing is the least of Bobby's habits… this… son of the social worker… Sue Doglas. Then he shifted his weight from one foot to the other, looking at his shoes, playing that guilty puppy look for all it was worth.

"I'm sorry Christine," he said.

"I want to believe you," she answered, but didn't sound like she did.

LATER ON, when I tell her they are just mocking her faith she looked genuinely surprised. "Why would anyone want to wear the shirt if they are not Christians? Just to mock Christians?"

We were heading home, the four of us. I didn't know what to say to her question. How do you answer that? It seemed like there was more to her question than mere naiveté, that she lived somewhere else where people were kind and good and gentle, that in that kingdom at least she was completely safe from all dangers. No one would mock the citizens by pretending to be a citizen. It was absurd. Unheard of. So by my raising the question, in her mind at least, it betrayed a weakness on my part to see people as they really were, happy citizens or…not. She thought I was simply being silly Eldon.

Yet while Kasie, James, Christine and I were walking, this Bobby ran up to her and tore off the shirt from his back, throwing it at her feet. He laughed at her, swore, basically saying it was just a joke on her. The shirt now had a curse by Jesus name on the shirt. I was about to raise my fist but she caught the slight movement of my hand and grasped my wrist.

"Don't draw attention to him. The Bible says 'A soft answer turns away wrath,'" she said firmly.

I wanted to hit him, I really did. But then it dawned on me. She was fully ready for his reaction. It didn't faze her.

I had half expected her to cry on our walk home, to seek comfort from Kasie, James or me, but that didn't happen. She just got quiet and by the time she was home she was over it. Her peace was already restored.

God sure protects this innocent of hers, I thought.I liked that innocence about her, but it could be exasperating at times. Still I suspected she had far more knowledge about the bad side of people and life than came across, with her happy mannerisms.

I looked at the sky and heard Christine's voice again, brought back to the present day. The day at school vanished; I'm back at the yacht "Grey Goose" again.

"What first drew you out here Old Salt? Was there a lady?"

Before Old Salt could answer a single swallow lighted upon the deck. He looked exhausted. Old Salt seemed relieved that Christine was distracted at this gasping swallow. Perhaps it was too private a question for him.

"Would you know the Happy Prince?" Christine asked the bird, cooing at it and reaching for it with her hands.

"That's a wild bird Christine. Best you don't touch it," Old Salt warned.

"Who is the Happy Prince?" I asked.

"He was a rich young and spoiled prince whom the Lord cursed to become a gilded statue. A single swallow came to the town and saw this very tall statue and did the statue favors, errands… in spite of the fact it was almost winter. Eventually the statue was stripped of all its gold as the swallow delivered these treasures to the very poor town's folk. It was a beautiful story."

"How does it end?" Kasie asked.

"You'll have to check the library. I can't remember every detail."

"I remember it. Oscar Wilde wrote this one," Old Salt said. "And I will tell the story now…"

"You remember it?" Kasie asked.

"Every word. I have it in my heart's memory."

"Then tell us!" Christine exclaimed.

"HIGH above the city, on a tall column, stood the statue of the Happy Prince. He was gilded all over with thin leaves of fine gold, for eyes he had two bright sapphires, and a large red ruby glowed on his sword-hilt."

He went on with this wonderful story, reciting the words without a flaw. Christine listened very intently. I was enjoying the sights of the shoreline passing, the towns, their harbors and bays, the beaches moving by us. I saw the craggy rocks near windswept sandy hillsides, another lighthouse and a tugboat to our right.

Then I heard again the voice of Old Salt,

"'I am glad that you are going to Egypt at last, little Swallow,' said the Prince. 'You have stayed too long here; but you must kiss me on the lips, for I love you.'

'It is not to Egypt that I am going,' said the Swallow. 'I am going to the House of Death. Death is the brother of Sleep, is he not?'

"And he kissed the Happy Prince on the lips, and fell down dead at his feet."

Christine's eyes watered a bit at this part, just a little. Kasie then looked away, embarrassed at her own reaction, she wiped away a tear from the corner of her eye and looked away to the sea. The sun and some dolphins riding along the cresting waves besides the yacht then distracted her. I got lost in watching these dolphins myself, and although Christine was also watching them, she heard every word of the story.

"'You have rightly chosen,' said God, 'for in my garden of Paradise this little bird shall sing for evermore, and in my city of gold the Happy Prince shall praise me.'"

Christine and Kasie both went, " Awwwww!" at that ending.

"Huh? I don't get it. That's it?" I asked confused. Kasie and Christine were laughing at the antics of the bouncy dolphins. I could see our harbor just a few yards away as the dolphins left us. Before we knew it the day's sail was over, we had pulled into the harbor and Old Salt went through the measures to ensure his yacht was safely docked, moored in and that the sails were properly tied down. He then drove us to the firehouse.

As we pulled in our parents, and a great scent of Smoky Franks "Hobo-stew" greeted us all. Supper that night was great. Our families found 'Smoky' Franks to be a very good host; he was talkative, well read, yet didn't go into debates over town politics as easily as the firemen did. Even Kasie enjoyed the supper, and had seconds on the ribs and stew as well. As Old Salt was with us, he was invited, and a few of the firemen also were at our table. Every time one or another of the younger fireman would bring up politics Old Salt or Smoky Franks would say "Pass the corn!" or "Pass the butter!" until they got the hint to change the subject.

Smoky pulled out a leather bound book. "Tom Bartlet just printed it up and I'm supposed to give you this. These are pictures of us vets from Apple Harbor, taken by that shutterbug Timothy Hophenetter."

While Christine's parents and mine both looked it over, he went on to explain that she had decided to print up about two hundred such books and sell them at the fundraiser.

"It has so many stories put here with the pictures," Mom remarked.

"I never knew Klanko was a gunner," Frank Solanski mentioned.

"Oh! I remember those stories Frank!" Emma Henderson

Solanski said. She had grown up in Apple Harbor after all.

"My father was with that company, the Black Panthers." Dad showed us his father's picture. I could see a lot of myself in his eyes, his youthful expression, but I had never met the man. The only pictures I had seen of him he looked tired.

"She wants to donate all profits to your fundraiser," Smoky explained to us.

" Why?" Frank asked Smoky. Always the skeptic.

He turned the pages to the very end of the book. Mr. Henderson was pictured with Timothy on this page. I saw a lot more words than were on the other pages. Mr. Henderson was in a hospital bed and Timothy was at his side. He was smiling, but Mr. Henderson wasn't. Dad read this part, and said, "I see..."

"What?" Mrs. Solanski asked him. "What?"

" I can certainly see why she wants to help the Hendersons," Dad said, having finally finished reading the entries.

" A lot of these guys will want to help if they knew this, if they were reminded," Christine's mom said after reading it herself. Then Frank shook his head in agreement as he read, saying, "That's for sure."

"WHAT?" Now us kids wanted to know. But they weren't talking.

****

"Mom, what was that book all about?" She was hanging laundry with the clothespins in her mouth. "Come on Ma, I really want to know."

"These clothes need to be hung before we get to church."

We lived on the second floor. Mom was hanging these clothes from the porch; we had a line that stretched far out over the parking lot. I liked the way the clothes were flapping in the breeze, the variety of bright colors and whites... it reminded me a lot of the sails and flags of Old Salt's yacht. They seemed to flow so easily, as if a part of the wind itself. I suddenly realized why Old Salt loved the sea. It calls you.

" Listen Mom, I'll help you, just talk to me."

I saw her brow furrow deeper, and the lines in her forehead rise up.

"I'm not sure she should have printed up that book!" she exclaimed.

Mom was working very fast. It was obvious she was very upset.

"Doesn't she think the poor man deserves some privacy?"

"Who Mom? Who are you talking about? Mr. Henderson? Mr. Hophenetter?"

"Now listen dear, you just get ready for church. I won't talk about it anymore," she said and added, "Well, except to say this. I'm mighty proud of you kids for how you're treating George."

" Thanks Mom. It's mostly Christine though. She likes that farm so much."

"She's a good girl."

"Mom, you ever go sailing?"

"Yeah, a time or two many years ago."

"You liked it?"

"Yeah, yeah I did. You enjoyed yourself then yesterday Eldon?"

"I had the time of my life Mom. I never knew sailing could be so cool!"

"Glad to hear it."

"Ma, I'll finish up. It'll take me no time to get a tie on."

"Really?"

"Yeah… clip-ons are great."

"You got your things packed for Wednesday morning?" Mom asked.

I would leave Wednesday for my Washington DC. trip. I knew what Mom was talking about.

"What's Wednesday Mom? Spaghetti day is it?"

"Yooouuu! DC., remember?!"

"It'll be done Tuesday night Ma."

In about five minutes I had the clothes and sheets hung up. I enjoyed this fresh air, and I swore I could hear the gulls and sounds of the tugboats sounding off again. The scream of bells from the fishing trawlers as the steam pressure would pierce through them and then… oh, yes… that sailing silence as we were in full sail. Oh, and way the waters were forever flowing beneath and all around us, bouncing and lapping into piles of froth and bubbles in their wake. I breathed in deep, and again I smelled the salty air and felt the wind break against my face. I knew I'd be out there again. I knew I'd again watch as buoys wobbled in the waves and seagulls made their beautiful sad song. The rocks and crags and sandy shores were just around the calendar somewhere, the waters were calling me, the winds were beckoning me home, like sirens with their long flowing manes singing their haunting melodies to sailors, I heard the song… I could not resist… *Come home*.

" Mariner… Mariner Old Salt…I understand you now. "

— chapter 12 —

Opposition Becomes Her Advertisement

When you live in Apple Harbor as long as I have you piece together conversations overheard in such a way they become something coherent, something solid. In this case, I overheard the following conversation at Tinti's that afternoon while I pretended to be napping at a booth.

Helen	"Christine is sooo quiet, I can't believe she could manage this."
Mrs. Doglas	"Quiet? She's Eldon's personal hyena. Laughing around him all the time. But you're so right. She never gives us the time of day. Some folks haven't heard her talk a peep for years! Must be mental like her mother!!"
Mrs. Wallstien	"What is she thinking? In these times of belt tightening around the community how could we help her uncle's farm out?"
Mrs. Doglas	"Well, we could pray for her to get some sense, I mean… guidance."
Mrs. Wallstien	"Certainly. We should all do that much for her."
Mrs. Doglas	"Prayer is a powerful thing you know."
Helen	"It might be fun to see what this young girl can do with the help of her friends and the churches."
Mrs. Doglas	"Helen Smhidt! That pastor John isn't even her

pastor! She attends the River of Life church, and you know how irresponsibly they handle the Word of God."

Mrs. Wallstien "Really?!"

Mrs. Doglas "The River of Life fill the youth with crazy ideas. And this girl is far too shy to do it. The first sign of opposition and she'll crumple like a dried up weed."

Mrs. Wallstien "That is a dangerous church. They go overboard when they are young, and when they're older they never come back to the faith. Remember Charlie Molt?"

They all got very quiet considering the tragic fate of this mysterious Charlie Molt.

Helen "Well, I agree she shouldn't try to involve the churches in her uncle's money problems, but still..."

Mrs. Wallstien "Precisely! We're not a charity board!"

Mrs. Doglas "Next she'll expect the churches to pay for her mother's hospital stay!"

Helen " Don't be mean now. I'm sure that's not on her agenda. Did you know Christine has the most wonderful grandmother?"

Mrs. Wallstien "Didn't Emma Solanski's husband just get reprimanded for..."

Helen "You know, Clarence is really putting on weight; it's a shame, he used to be a handsome man. Maybe he should stop eating so much chow mien."

Mrs. Doglas "His wife is a good cook. You used to have a thing for Clarence, didn't you Helen? Come on, you're with friends here!"

I knew this conversation wouldn't get any better, it never did. I wondered if gossip was outlawed whether their tongues would atrophy from lack of use? I felt sorry for them. Especially Helen

Smhidt. I stretched and yawned loudly, leaving the booth and got up to pay for my coffee. Babbs smiled at me as she wiped her hands on her apron in front of the old cash register.

"Honey, you know I can still remember when I saw your sister and Christine first come in here. That girl must've been four years old. A head full of waves and the bluest eyes, and you were always doing something funny to make her laugh."

" You mean Christine? Like what Babbs? I remember when she was a child she hardly ever spoke at all," I said, finding this lady's words like a fireplace for the soul.

"You brought a dead cat to Show and Tell that you kept in a cardboard box. You didn't get called on that first day, so you left the box under your desk until it stunk up the whole room. You were a funny kid. They had to air out that class the whole morning."

"Who told you that?" I asked Babbs.

"Besides Christine? She sure laughed telling me that one! Your former teacher, Mrs. Hophenetter, it happened in her class, six or seven years ago I guess, when she was last teaching."

"I forgot about that. I'm helping people move some stuff out of their homes for the fundraiser, Fred and a few others. Hopefully nothing too heavy!"

"Christine also told me you used to balance on pipes which crossed the river, and one day you came to her church after your services and you two went to that pipe. She said you fell in your newest suit. Whatever possessed you son?"

"I hated wearing ties," I said, only half joking. I never expected I would have fallen in. I had balanced across there a hundred million times in a week's time. Christine simply used the bridge, which was only thirty feet away. I remember we were sitting under that big oak tree; I was wiping mud off my face. She didn't say much. She never did. But she was laughing; I think she was eleven years old. She wore a pretty spring dress, checkered blue with a white blouse. Her laughter was more like the breezes of spring, which flowed through the tall grasses, instead of the noise I heard from schoolmates. She was extremely gentle, quiet and sensitive. I had said to her, "I'm the creature from the lagoon of Apple Harbor!" which earned me more laughter and genuine smiles. Even then I felt well recompensed. But as she clamed up around others so much, most folks never saw that side of her.

Lost in those thoughts, I went to Butch's Garage and saw the guys looking over the hood of a 1952 Chevy Deluxe. I had no idea at the time it was Mr. Rowe's car, but it looked like a nice car. I love the grill, the shape. It looks strong, like a hunter green tank.

Butch said, "Those quilters sure are getting on my nerves. Mabel went and called my wife last night trying to get her to join up. That'll be the day."

Russ Peters said, "Yeah? You let her go there and you might as well talk to the lawyers if you know what I mean."

Otto, one of three of Russ's brothers, agreed.

Judge Parker just looked amused, he didn't say anything until Russ asked him if Mabel had called there too.

"Yep, she sure did. She called about something else too you might want to know."

Mr. Mays, a quiet man, broke in. "It wouldn't happen to be about the Henderson farm now would it?"

Butch, who was holding a water pump in his left hand and a dirty rag in the right looked at me and smiled. "Hey kid. What do you know about this Henderson farm, besides its being in trouble?"

"I think we should help it out," I said in earnest.

Otto Peters, who was looking under the hood for no reason at all, said, "I agree, as does my Kelly. She says we need to take care of each other whenever we can."

"Farming isn't easy anywhere now, with the prices the Wallstein's Elevator gave us," Butch complained.

Butch still farmed some, but he had always had the shop, a second full-time job. That wasn't uncommon unfortunately.

I looked at the engine of the Deluxe, it was scattered everywhere. I couldn't tell what Butch was doing, because it seemed whenever I got there a circle of visitors assembled. He'd have a socket wrench in his hand while the boys would talk quiet emotionally about road conditions, local politics, their son's games and the school board. A guy could wait twenty minutes to ask for an estimate while Butch was arguing with a guy who lost his car keys, and another guy who wanted to know if he wanted to play darts tonight. It drove some guys absolutely crazy waiting.

Of course, there were plenty of magazines around, piles and piles of them. Mostly boring shop magazines that they sent him, a few hunter and various sport magazines. He didn't subscribe to half of them. I saw guys waiting in the one chair in the corner by the keys and water cooler, where trash and new parts were scattered about, between old parts and receipts at Butch's desk. After about four or five customers were waiting in a line Butch would suddenly spring to action, and the meeting of the minds broke up. But sometimes it'd take awhile for those meetings to break up.

Butch's voice brought me back to the present day.

"Well Eldon, you know I've got an empty water bottle in the back, why don't you go get a paper, some tape and a marker. Label it 'HENDERSON FUND'. What do you think?"

"I think that is an awesome idea!" I shouted, and I quickly labeled the water bottle as he asked.

As I was doing so I overheard Mr. Mays ask Butch where he could get a spare bottle like that, and Randy Nelson said, "I have plenty at my shop."

I hadn't even noticed Mr. Nelson around before. Then I overheard the Weinrich brothers say they could donate some meat if… IF there was a fundraiser. They ran the Meat Locker right by Mays Hobby and Curiosity Shop.

"I think collecting a few quarters around town might help out a little," Mr. Mays said. "We might come up with some more ideas later. That's why you're here, right Eldon? To help your friends?"

I just smiled back, then thanked them, and left for James place. We would leave with his dad to collect things around town to sell at the potential fundraiser. I had my doubts about that.

These conversations we overheard while helping out with that moving… people do have more than one phone in their homes you know. James and I were moving stuff from people's homes into the Sunny Valley Baptist church's storage garage, and when we heard people say, "Oh Lord, it's that Wallstein woman!!" We picked up the other line to listen. Sometimes with their knowledge, sometimes not.

"Fred, I can't believe you'd go along with that Solanski girl."

"Who is this?"

"Mabel Wallstien."

There was silence for a long time, then an audible sigh.

"It's only polite to say who you are when you call people Mabel."

"Well?"

"Well what? Her idea isn't really all that bad," Fred said.

"She's only fourteen years old, did you see her give that talk?"

"So, she was nervous, so what? The idea is to have a few area churches use the Town Green. I for one don't have a problem with that. She has five area pastors she talked to that are behind doing a fundraiser. It's her idea. Not her project."

"They'll have Smoky Franks there." Mrs. Wallstien sounded genuinely alarmed.

"Burgers too I hope?"

"You're joking about that? You know old Smoky? That homeless guy."

"Oh, Duane Franks. Yeah, he'll help out with the fundraiser, so what?"

"Well, don't you wonder what sort of criminal elements he'll bring?"

"Not really, you know why Mabel?"

"No?"

"I know you'll be there."

When Fred hung up he yelled, "James, you can hang up now too." We then sheepishly showed up downstairs. Fred showed James where some more empty boxes were to gather stuff from his workroom, attic and basement. "It'll have yellow tags on it if it's meant to go boys. Thanks so much for this."

I had to smile. " No, thank you Fred! Thank you! This will mean a lot to the Hendersons."

" Yeah, it's nice junk," James said. "I mean..."

" It's not junk either," he told James.

CALL TWO

"Helen, I heard they'll have criminal elements at the fundraiser."

"What fundraiser?"

"That Solanski... Scranski girl's fundraiser... whatever her name is."

"You mean for the Henderson barn?"

"Yes for the Hendersons. That homeless guy is going to be there."

"Perhaps I should send out petitions or a protest letter to the editor."

(Mabel could pick up on the sarcasm in Helen's voice.)

"Well, people have a right to know."

"I suppose. What else is on your mind? If anything's there at all." Helen sighed.

"They'll be breaking the law, separation of church and state laws."

"How do you figure that Mabel?"

"Five of our area churches are involved in this fundraiser."

"You know what Mabel? I think perhaps you should simply drop this!"

"But you want those Hendersons to... that Christine... uh..."

"Christine? I won't touch that one. She's nice," Helen explained.

"Helen? I don't get it, what's with you all of a sudden?"

"Well maybe you never met her charming grandmother."

And Helen laughed. It was a real laugh from deep within her.

Mabel didn't understand this whatsoever!

"WHO is this grandmother I keep hearing so much about?"

"I'll go with you tonight to the town meeting, for the sake of thirty-five years of friendship. But maybe we're on the wrong side of this one."

"Nonsense Helen!"

Then Helen seemed to realize something they had in common and she changed the subject altogether. "Oh, did you hear about Brian Lenkey, Mabel? I heard..."

After she got off the phone Mrs. Smhidt showed us which things to collect. There wasn't a junky looking thing among them. That surprised me the most.

Helen Smhidt didn't smile, she growled and fussed, saying, "I meant to get rid of this junk for years!!" So maybe it had nothing whatsoever to do with the cow of human kindness here being milked. But whatever the reasons, I liked it.

* * * * *

Now, about Mrs. Hophenetter...

Word spread quickly in the small town that Mrs. Hophenetter had left her house. From Crachet's Barber Shop, where the Nelson's high school boys had mentioned it to Russ Peters and Bobby O'Brien, who were playing their eternal card game years before they retired, to Hattie Olstien who was good friends with Mrs.Wallstien and had the story confirmed by Mr. Mays, who considered this a sign of happy things to come, and the story would have stopped there were it not for Mrs. Hophenetter herself. For she kept showing up, in Mrs. Crayfish's 'Cut Loose' Beauty Parlor, Mr. Mays' Hobby and Curiosity Shop, Tinti's Restaurant; she drew the attention of the young Nelson twins, seven -year-olds Gary and Harold at their father's hardware store, right next to Mays'. So of course by Monday the whole of Willis School knew about this strange lady who wears winter coats to buy thumb screws and asks for a fountain drink, whatever that is.

"And yes, she used to be a teacher once years and years ago!" The kids would say, when it was only six or seven years ago.

And at Tom Bartlet's printing shop Heather Anson was seen smiling at Mrs. Hophenetter as if she knew the Midnight Gardener her whole life. A few people saw her at Old Salt's. The one who was spreading stories the most was Helen Smhidt. She wasn't sure of what to make of Mrs. Hophenetter's 'return', and didn't want to lose any edge, or advantage.

Helen knew that Mrs. Hophenetter could use that book to her

advantage at the next city council. The first order of the city town council's meeting was the very proposal of holding the benefit for the Henderson's. None other than Mrs. Hophenetter quickly put out the motion to decide the outcome of the fundraiser on the Green.

"This is intolerable!" Mrs. Wallstien shouted, and said a bunch of incoherent things about Apple Harbor becoming a welfare center for all sorts of losers who couldn't make it on their own. She went on and on about how this is a fiscally conservative town, that in the end "this will bankrupt us and our grandchildren down to the forth generation," and how it would "force religion down the throats of our innocent children and teens."

James and I laughed out loud at that one. We tried to not laugh out loud, but the harder we tried the more the build-up came until pretty much everyone in the place decided Mrs. Wallstien was wrong about us teens being all that innocent.

She still pressed on with "risks of allowing public grounds to be used for stupid religious purposes." She lost her audience there. Helen rolled her eyes. She had nothing to say to that, as she loved her church. Nearly everyone in that meeting attended one church or another, for whatever our faith was, these were God-fearing people. Or at the very least God acknowledgers.

"Look, it's not just about religion here," Mrs. Wallstien tried another tactic. " But about allowing large groups of people to use our public lands for there own personal use. I think we should carefully reconsider this, perhaps put it to another vote later this summer after a committee has looked over all the ramifications. Let's not be hasty after all."

Mrs. Wallstein looked ready to bust a gasket when Judge Parker slammed his hammer down, indicating her time was up. Somehow she kept her peace. Judge Parker looked at her and, unconscious of the fact he was shaking his head at her in disbelief. He tried to be impartial but still, she just got to him with that 'it's not about religion here.' That took the cake. She looked at everyone in the town hall and said, "I haven't hardly started!" and Judge Parker groaned back. "Mabel, you haven't shut up about this since you walked in the door, everyone knows how you feel and I think our mayor has something to say… I'd like to add I respect your contributions to the town, you've had a good many wonderful ideas." He sighed and groaned. " Some not so wonderful."

So Judge Parker, the head of the city council, gave the mayor his ten minutes to talk. The mayor gave that time to a short old lady no one remembered seeing before, except… a few thought she looked familiar.

"Hello." The old lady looked at everyone and shook her head in disappointment.

"I happen to know that many of you people here owe your very lives to George Henderson. I have a copy of a letter Mrs. Hophenetter was so kind as to loan me."

That soft old voice sounded like a voice we all knew, but couldn't place. Someone we lost years ago maybe, but had always kept in the back folders of our mind.

"'My love, my lady'," the lady went on. "'Apple Harbor's own George Henderson risked his neck for a good many of us on the night of June 10, 1944. We were caught in a terrible crossfire, surrounded by Nazis from all sides. I won't go into all the details of it except to say we had given ourselves up as lost. Now George Henderson was wingman in a squad of fighters, and when he heard the base radio report that reinforcements were needed for the Black Panthers, he quickly broke formation and single-handedly took on a tank division by many risky swoops and dives, which diverted their attention and drew much of their fire upon himself. He took out many of their troops by strafe fire, and he destroyed two enemy tanks by simply drawing their fire on him. The result was in their positions; in the confusion they destroyed each other. Two tanks caught exposed, one with its engine stalled, and in opposing positions.

"My Sgt. Smhidt was seriously wounded, and if it weren't for the bravery of George Henderson, I know none of us would have survived that battle. But within the few minutes of his diverting them, we received reinforcements, supplies, and were able to destroy their tanks and personnel. My men, among them Nelson, Roman, Anderson, Parker, Murphy, Wallstien, Franks and Sgt. Smhidt all owe their lives to the man now facing a court martial.

"His plane was shot down and he was badly burned in his legs, but fortunately a division north of us was able to pull him and his gunner out before the canopy of his plane was consumed.

"He broke rank and is considered a deserter by the army brass. But not all the brass shares these sentiments, so I guess I'm asking you to pray for the outcome honey. The good Lord saved our necks, and George got pretty banged up in the bargain.

"Love you, Tim

"Captain Hopheneter, US Army somewhere in France, July 2, 1944'.

"Now people, you heard it from my lips first. You all owe this man a lot. Excuse me, I don't mean to carry on so." The old woman was crying. She regained her composure after a moment and went on.

"I happen to know that that squadron had some other names in it, you'll see it in Mrs. Hophenetter's book if you have the sense God gave you to look! You… Mr. Anson, your daddy was there, and you Hank, you were with that squadron, Russ and Bob… glad to see you here. I know you were in that particular battle. Ain't I right?"

People didn't know what to say. As the old lady hobbled back to her seat next to Officer Frank Solanski everyone wondered, but no one asked… who was she? For that yellowed old note read by a very passionate old woman had changed everyone's mind. That note itself had decided the vote, and the people voted for the benefit. Even Helen smiled at the outcome, as she walked over to say "Hello" to her new friend Debbie Andrews.

The town voted to let a committee decide how to handle this. Our hearts sank at this, but an inner prompting comforted us with the sense that we should simply 'Be Still and Know I am God,' that somehow things might work out.

* * * * *

Right after that meeting Kasie and I were called to help Mr. Henderson move the horses into one of his storage barns that he had converted into stables. Now all they needed to worry about was the chickens. The geese, pigs and sheep were all taken care of.

We covered their eyes with the blinders as we walked them into the trailer, and then Mr. Henderson closed the trailer door. There was plenty of hay in the trailer. He talked to his horses just before we headed down the dirt road to his farm. I mentioned that road which has apple trees on one side, and maple trees on the other. Already they were in full bloom, and you could tell we were at the farm by the glow of the whitewash on the trees, and that fresh scent of wet maple buds after that rain we had that day.

I wondered where Christine was; this was her favorite part of visiting the farm, the horses.

When we got the horses settled, I saw what a makeshift arrangement this was. There were all kinds of wires running through theses flimsy boards used to stable these horses. But for now this would work. Only Jake was kept in the strongest stable of all, which was not reinforced particleboards but a well built oak stable. At least he had carefully checked for loose wires and pulled them in tight and secure.

We closed the gates, and after a bit of petting the mare and Midnight Cry, we made to leave, except we saw that old lady again. She was leaving the farmhouse with Officer Solanski. She walked straight to the horses with a quick greeting to us. She knew our names. Kasie walked out to the pick-up.

The old lady went up to the loft and sat down in the hay. Kasie was waiting for Mr. Henderson for our ride home, so I was about to leave.

But then I heard the lady pray in Christine's voice…

"So Lord… You were born in a place really like this, huh? How blessed are those beasts, these animals to have been able to share in that! It makes me all quiet inside to consider how humble You must be, how gentle. I mean barns don't exactly smell like roses and here You are, the King of the Universe being born in a stinky old barn. I'd love You God for that reason alone!

"I'm feeling really torn about this acting assignment. I didn't have to lie today but still I feel uncomfortable with what happened to Mrs. Smhidt. I'm asking You to please cover me there; I really need You to show me how to make that right. You don't want us to lie.

"Please help my Uncle George and Aunt Betty in this situation. I know You have before Lord. You are truly, truly the most beautiful hearted Happy Prince I know... Love you lots."

I tried to get away before she came down again, having invaded that space I felt kind of bad. But she was down in just a moment's time, as I waited for her "AMEN" but never heard it I didn't expect she was done.

I could see she was crying, but smiling all at the same time.

"Eldon, He sure loves us. He does."

I gave her a side hug, putting my arm around her shoulder. I walked her with her that way until we got to her father's car, then I gave her a hug and said, " I'm so glad you're a Christian CHRISTINE." I laughed.

I couldn't believe she had done something like this! Who was this Christine after all? Did I really know her, even after nine years?

When I got back to Mr. Henderson's truck Kasie asked me, "You make it a habit to try to pick up old ladies?"

Mr. Henderson snorted at that, and we never tried to explain it to her.

— chapter 13 —

Letters and Interviews

Eldon,

You asked for a letter from me.
Here it is...

B

Your crazy bro,
James.

PS: Please don't start a rogue government while you're in Washington, DC. We need you here for baseball even if you choke every time Lisa happens to be anywhere near you (on planet earth.)

* * * * *

Hello Son,

Make sure you take lots of pictures when you're gone. Dress warm. Don't get lost. When you take a shower use soap on your body.

I love you, Mom.

* * * * *

Hi Eldon!

I hope you are having fun in Washington DC as you tour and visit your cousins in Virginia, even if you really don't know them all that well and 'they talk goofy, dress funny and basically seem odd' as you said it. Be patient with them, okay? It seems weird with you gone, James and Randy really look out of sorts and can hardly carry a baseball all that well.

I have to admit that Kasie's one unique girl, that's for sure. Not too many people I know who paint their rooms concord grape purple! Don't worry about your room. I heard that your father stopped her before she finished painting all the walls and that the white paint is pretty much covering up the grapey color. Now it's a faded purple like a pastel flower. Maybe we could paint it with marigolds, or lilies. (Just kidding!).

Kasie broke the porch window again trying to dribble a basketball down the stairs. "Third time the charm," was all she could say when your father found out. Your dad is making her pay for it out of the paper route, so now she has to do that alone, except James and I keep her company.

She's better at stopping on skates than I am.

But the dogs listen to me. I got them listening to me! I do that on my own.

You won't believe this. Our fundraiser has made the papers.

I don't mean advertisements. I mean several ladies wrote these letters protesting the committee's handling of the fundraiser vote. They're mad at it because they think churches should be allowed to use the Green. The committee has buried the vote pretty much, which I expected. Well over half of the letters were in favor of the churches doing this. People talk about this at Tinti's and at school! I've had four teachers ask me about the fundraiser, of course I refer them to one of the churches that are sponsoring it.

Even Mom is getting all sorts of questions at her work about 'Christine's fundraiser'. I wish they wouldn't call it that. Still, it's funny how so many people seem to have read those protest letters in the paper, now they want to go to it to see what the fuss is all about. It is interesting how God worked this one out!

I had an hour to walk the trails today. I got a lot of grief at school about this... "event that Christine couldn't see through," so I needed this. We are promised tribulation and grief, as Christians aren't we?

This might sound silly but I could see the affection God has for us in the very leaves. Even in the varieties of dirt. I guess I should explain that instead of just saying that so abruptly!

I think you understand that Eldon, as you seem to always be drawing trees and you understand the need to see details. Nature has a way of grabbing my attention because God poured Himself into its works. Nature doesn't fully express our need for forgiveness of course, but that's a different matter.

I see His affectionate nature among budded maples and those green birch trees. I couldn't believe the details He put into weeds and the stuff most people will never see so much artistry in such tiny things. So fantastic! What an intricate and vast mind!

I touched so many leaves, grabbed handfuls of dirt, crushed seeds, and looked all around me in a dizzying maze just in a effort to feel closer to this great MIND. It's as if everything came fresh from the etchings, so much to see. I saw tiny grapevines delicately wrapped around a young oak, with an abandoned blue bird's nest. But who sees these things? I gasped at the glory of it! Nature has a beauty that can hardly be contained even now.

Craig and Michael Balligrino saw me out there but didn't say anything. They just looked at me funny but I didn't know anyone was around. I wish they wouldn't find satisfaction in such foolish things. Of course I must have looked very foolish to them as I was grabbing leaves and seeds while enjoying everything.

I cried for them in my prayers tonight.

Lately God is teaching me to rely on his strength, I'm learning. Pray that God gives Mom and me wisdom and puts the right words in our mouths, should anyone ask us questions about the fundraiser.

God Bless you richly as you have been a source of encouragement and support for me.

Take care,
Your sister in Christ,
Christine

* * * * *

Hi everyone, (except Mom or Dad/ separate note)

Sorry this is a group letter but... the bus trip to Washington DC. wasn't entirely awful; I mean I had the option of staying with family members instead of a motel with 60 other carriers and two adult chaperones. I probably got a good half-hour more sleep than any of them that first night. It seems like the whole idea of a trip like this was to go crazy. That seems to be how these guys acted on the bus anyways.

These girls were away from home for the very first time in their lives, crying on the bus as if we were going to a funeral or something. They were awfully young, about twelve. One girl even cried out, "There's no turning back now!" as the bus pulled out.

There were also some kids who really didn't miss their houses whatsoever.

So, of course in order to appear tough and together Balligrino's goon squad had kept some bottles of beer between them, hidden in the lining of their coats. They always sat in the back of the bus to play cards, do their drinking and harass and intimidate everyone they considered their inferior. Which made up half the bus at the time.

If Pastor John only knew his boys choir is made up of idiots.

Still, in all, it wasn't too bad. They didn't light the motel on fire and were quiet within an hour after lights were out at the motel, I was told. I couldn't say the same about my cousin's place.

My cousin Johnny, who was just two at last summer's family reunion, was up all night puking his guts out over a turkey dinner. I missed that reunion because of my paper route and the one in 1972 because I got lost in the woods while hiking with James, who said he had a compass but all he had really was a can of spam.

I won't let you forget that James, ever!

We were only lost for six hours, you'd think by everyone's reactions we were gone for six weeks. How a person could confuse a can of spam for a compass is beyond me.

So now I can hardly take a walk down the hall without some relative or other saying to me, "Don't get lost, don't get lost," except for Kasie who says, "Go ahead, get lost." I'm not sure but I think I procrastinated my paper route that day last summer on purpose, sort of a fried-slip or something. I love my gram, my Aunt Emma, my cousins in Apple Harbor, but I sure am tired of hearing about my one time getting lost so many years ago. I hiked hundreds of times since and hadn't gotten lost. But no one ever mentioned that to you James even once. (Note the green jealous creature lurking behind you...payback's coming bro.)

This trip was good for me. My Aunt Joanne and Uncle Mark hardly noticed me at all with their kids, seven at home still. I'm sure my mom sent a detailed letter explaining various instructions, but I didn't notice any weird restrictions. They had no TV but that wasn't as bad as it sounds. There were lots of activities, and after I got over my own concerns about being around them, I found I really liked these cousins.

I wrestled with the boys, learned some different games, Kelly brought me samples of her cooking but I liked Joey's better. Oh, then there is... Ruth. I read to her, she is five. I read to her a lot this week in the late afternoons, when my group isn't touring the Capitol, the Smithsonian, or the White House. All in all I had more fun with them than I did seeing a bunch of marble blocks.

The cherry blossoms were nice along the Jefferson Memorial, but we have that at home on our green. Our bus group did get to see Jefferson's mansion Monticello. But I'll remember my cousins more than anything.

Your friend,
Eldon.

* * * * *

Home. When the bus pulled into the station, Dad, Mom and Kasie were waiting. It was pretty late, somewhere around ten p.m. by the time we got my luggage out from under the bus luggage compartments.

"Oh, how I hate the smell of diesel fuel," my mom complained.

I loved that smell. It reminded me of the many free rides I took through my uncle's route, up through Apple Harbor, down through the valley and all the way into New Haven then back.

"About Christine's project Eldon…"

"HMMMM?"

"It's run into a bit of a snag," Dad said.

Kasie added, "The churches are fighting over the timing of it all and each one says they won't take part unless they have domm domm, what's that word Dad?"

"Unless they have first dibs Kasie. They want to all do it on THEIR CHURCH property."

"But the barn itself is almost completed. It just needs paint."

"I wonder why this project is so important to Christine anyhow?" Mom asked us.

"You really don't know?" Kasie said.

"Well… no, I don't."

" I'm glad she's involved, but the barn is built."

I thought Mom would get an answer to her unasked question, but Kasie never said anything more on the subject. She shot a look at Kasie who just shrugged her shoulders acting like the whole thing was too obvious to deserve an answer.

"They could lose the farm because of debts honey," Dad finally answered,

" And because…" He never finished his thought.

Then I put my travel-pillow on my suitcase and caught a fifteen-minute nap.

* * * * *

The next morning on our way to school Kasie and Christine were talking about love. James and I kept quiet. Some conversations could get you in trouble.

"Love is roses and chocolate, lace and candles and walks on the lane," Kasie said.

"I think love is finding someone to change diapers and decades with," Christine replied.

"Love is when he cuddles with you and tells you how beautiful you are!" Kasie sighed.

"Love is when he puts up with your stupid skating shows and occasionally watches them with you, and you watch those dumb westerns with him."

"Love is flowers for no reason."

"Love is the ability to see a beauty as the leathering of the skin rolls around into the joints and marrow, and some clown has etched lines and burrows all over his face. He still makes you laugh as he hides your teeth before an important speech. Love is migraines and losing jobs, but holding on anyways."

"Love, isn't it laces and…" Kasie sounded heartbroken.

"Braces and love can hurt. Love can be painful. My grandmother used to say love makes you vulnerable, you're so open but she also said there is nothing better in this life. Or worse. Be wise she said in those matters of the heart." Christine didn't sound jaded, only grounded.

"What else did your grandma say about love Christine?" Kasie asked.

"That the greatest reward of marriage is seeing the fruit of the vine ripen; the love blossom as a couple recognizes the seasons of marriage, its ebbs and flow. You know like the tide… she said love has to take out the sea's impurities and bring in fresh waters. She said by His grace I would stay the course with my husband someday."

"That's an interesting way to look at it," Kasie answered. " I think of my love as a prince and how he'll carry me off someday."

"Maybe like a lion would?" James asked.

"Ohhh, what do you know?"

"No, Kasie… a lion. My prince is like an untamed Lion, like Aslan. I love how my prince will rescue me even before I know I need it. At least that's how I imagine him to be. Tough, manly, strong, confident, yet tender as a lamb."

"Lamb is about as dumb a creature you could get, and boy does it stink!" James laughed.

"There's hope for you yet then James!" Kasie replied teasing. She lightly punched his arm, grinning at her own joke.

"A baby, a lamb is so gentle. In Jesus' day the young women had lambs as pets. Perhaps when Jesus was born the shepherds presented Mary with a young lamb. You never know," Christine explained to us.

"Well Christine, not to change the subject but..."

"I was done anyhow Kasie."

"Our pastor called again about picking up some more things after school."

"Your Pastor Axworthy?"

"Yes."

"I met the man. He seems kind. Where are we to..."

James interrupted her, "Who said anything about we?"

"Well, James, it seems to me you had your fun on the biplane, and his antique car, and all the meals her aunt has given you; we're just asking you to help load a few boxes," Kasie said clearly very irritated with James.

"This whole thing is pretty selfish of Christine if you think about it."

"What do you mean James?" Christine asked him, looking a bit hurt at his remarks, especially when he was he talking about her as if she wasn't there.

" It's your aunt and uncle's farm. It's your family."

"So?"

"There you are."

"James," I said. " Do what you want to do. But I'd appreciate your help. I don't see anything all that selfish in her wanting to help family."

"I'd like your company James but if you decide to not help that's fine. You're always my friend, OK?" Christine was smiling a genuine smile, from her heart. She was walking backwards to his walk, looking him straight in the eyes with her right arm extended to his shoulder.

" I haven't decided anything yet."

A couple of hours later, in between classes I ran into James.

"What was that all about bro?"

" It's nothing. Kasie won't be helping either. We're tired of the talk, that's all."

After that chewing out Kasie gave James, that shocked me. But I tried to convince him nevertheless...

"James, after having swung a bat into the players dugout twice last year I didn't figure you'd care what people would say!"

He wouldn't say anything so I said, "Okay. Maybe afterwards I'll see you at your softball practice."

He was a great pitcher but a lousy hitter.

* * * * *

Meanwhile, on the farm that reporter from the Gazette was trying to find George Henderson, who was too busy to know she wanted to find him. He was in the garage repairing the biplane's engine to prepare it for crop dusting, so he didn't hear her drive up. When she knocked on the farmhouse door Mrs. Henderson offered to let her inside, but the reporter said she needed to see Mr. Henderson right away.

"He's in that garage then. Don't take up too much of his time, we got work to do."

She said, pointing her way.

"It won't be but a few minutes."

"Mr. Henderson?" She peeked through the partly opened door.

"Hmm?"

"I'm... Audrey Kuspert, from the *Apple Harbor Gazette*, and I was at there when the elderly woman gave a very good talk on your behalf last week at the town hall meeting."

Mr. Henderson put his wrench down, rubbed the grease from his hands and looked at her, smiling. He pushed his white bangs back from his forehead, smearing small dabs of grease there, and placed the tools in his overall pockets.

"That would be my niece, Miss Kus..."

"Kuspert. She looked old enough to be your mother."

"It was my niece Christine."

She eyed Mr. Henderson very skeptically.

"I wanted to know about your war experiences."

His smile disappeared. He put his hands back in his pockets, reaching for his wrenches, and looked away from her, returning to his work.

" I have work to do Miss."

"It's about that day on June 10, 1944 when you..."

"Goodbye. You need to leave now."

She waited a moment, hoping for more, but he had clamed up. It was obvious he wasn't going to talk about it. As she walked away she said, "I can probably get the story from another source, perhaps that niece of yours?"

"You just better leave my niece out of that paper of yours, you hear me?" He shouted throwing down his tools to the floor.

"I could Mr. Henderson."

"I don't like the way you said that."

"Well, a niece who dresses up to look old might make a good story, and she could help me fill in some of the blanks."

"Christie don't know nothing."

"Doesn't know anything you mean? Then I could fill in the blanks myself."

He didn't like this woman before, now she was correcting his grammar. And just what did she mean by saying she'd fill in the blanks?

"I'd get you for libel or harassment."

"I doubt that. It would make you look like the hero. Every word would be true, I'd simply find other sources. Besides, this story could gain you sympathy for raising support for that fundraiser."

"Listen Miss Kuspert, war isn't your social gathering to play bridge or darts and I sure don't appreciate you trying to dig this stuff out of me again. Let the dog lie on this one, trust me, will you? I don't really care one way or the other about a fundraiser anyways, I'm not going to milk my neighbors for money."

"I'm sorry. I'm not trying to uncover anything painful out of this; I just wanted a story from you. Something very simple."

"How simple?"

"I wanted to hear you recount that day for my readers."

For the longest time he said nothing, then… the story came out of its own accord. Like it needed a place to land.

"I can remember seeing young bodies of boys in the German fields. You know they have farms very much like this one in Germany? I wasn't always in the air you know. I got shot down twice and survived. But that particular day was my last time up. I remember hearing about the Black Panther Squadron on Charlie's radio. That's half of the men of Apple Harbor. No, I wasn't going to just ignore that, they were under heavy fire and they were only five minutes' flight north of my co-ordinates. I dived those tanks, drew their fire and dived again, finishing off some of the German ground troops. I must've done that about five or six times. I saw they had reinforcements and were okay. As I was returning to join my squadron I was shot down."

"Why be ashamed of that?"

"We lost two planes when I abandoned my wing. That's nothing to be proud of. I was almost court marshaled for it and my legs were caught in the fire so I lost my wings."

"Thank you Mr. Henderson."

"So is that enough? You got your story?"

"Yes. Just one other question. Would you do it again? Knowing what you know now, would you still shoot at the enemy?"

"Without a doubt. I don't lose sleep over that. Just the two downed planes."

When she drove off he sighed and grumbled, "What a day. On top of this how am I to explain to Betty I was trying to shoot that stupid rat that was bothering the chickens and I got her pet rooster Cogburn instead?"

— chapter 14 —

Last Hurdle?

The sun seemed extra eager to get up these days, as if it had something to get up for. I was folding the papers and noticed a story on the Town Section about Mr. Henderson. It was interesting. It had an old file picture of him when the police questioned him about four years ago at his farm for flying low downtown. It wasn't the best photograph ever taken of him, it looked as if he was having some kind of seizure, and his hair was a terrible crow's nest from having just stepped out of the biplane. He was having a sneezing fit, for he was allergic to the herbicides he had sprayed and that was the moment Mabel Wallstein took his photograph. She tried to capture the essence of the man, and yet with every click of the lens he'd pop out another explosion, and after about six tries she figured she must have caught him looking somewhat normal during the intermission between sneeze and relief. She was simply filling in for the *Apple Harbor's Journal Courier's* full time photographer, Eugene Morrison. It was only a hobby to her, and a very short-lived one at that.

The article on Mr. Henderson wasn't very kind. It went on about how he was manipulating his war record to gain sympathy from the good people of Apple Harbor, and how he was almost court marshaled. It raised more questions than it did information. Why wasn't the court marshal carried out? Who did he know, that kind of thing. But this article was from the competitor of Mrs. Kuspert. She had kept her word, her article was kind.

While I was browsing through that article, my eyes scanned down to another article, only a paragraph long, titled "Young Woman

Disguises Herself For Family Farm." It was about Christine, but it didn't name her by name. In those days you couldn't do that unless you had committed some hideous crime, but what was the use of committing the crime if you couldn't even get your picture in the paper? You had to be an adult to do that. Half of those lucky adults captured on film looked worse than Mr. Henderson sneezing, they didn't even know how to put their jackets on right, it seemed half of them wore jackets on their heads as they were led to the courthouse.

I decided right then and there, after reading the part of the article... "...how the unnamed youth had been thoroughly corrupted by her uncle into misleading the good citizens of Apple Harbor", that I would neglect part of my duties as a paperboy. I would make sure none of my customers received the first page of the TOWN section, and instead I would insert a mimeographed copy of a drawing I did, which was not very kind of Mrs. Wallstien. I didn't label the drawing as such. In this drawing she was having a terrible sneezing fit and I'm sure your imagination can fill in the details.

Yes, the sun was bright and cheery this morning, and as I was roller-skating over the cobblestones in the back of Mays' Hobby store, I caught a whiff of the bakery in all its glory. You know the first thing in the morning when the only creatures that are about are dogs and deliverymen, and the sugar fog comes out of the grates and floods the air with its warm, fresh-out-of-the-oven bread scents, then it's ohhhh, yes, the jelly rolls which linger in the air like a finger of aroma, it sent me into the door of the bakery in no time.

Even the doors of the Sweetheart Bakery had those bells.

"Hello?" I called out, trying to steady myself as I balanced in the doorway.

"Yes? Oh hi Eldon. You look quite white today." It was Christine, sitting at a table with her father.

I looked at myself and saw that as I skated through the fog coming from the grates, I had lingered too long.

Melva asked me what I wanted, I asked for a Bismarck, two jellyrolls, and a bread roll. Then I very cautiously skated over to Christine's booth.

"So, you wanna hear about some miracles... Well, I should start off by saying that North View is like a big ongoing miracle. The feeling of love and unity is incredible and a miracle in itself." Christine was talking about a Christian camp she went to last year.

"Go on."

"Like I was saying before, it's just like in Acts, that whole summer, it was just like the book says, I was in a constant state of awe. And right now, I mean just thinking about it I get that complete intense feeling, just as if I were there." Her hands were emphasizing her words.

"Because you see, when I went to North View I found a reality to God's kingdom that was sooo real and I took it home. It hasn't gone away yet. But I'm not talking about feelings here, I mean... there God's glory was right in front of me for two months straight. It's as if I just whispered His name, I would hear a response immediately after."

"You can't stay in a constant state of awe honey. North View is your little vacation from reality. It just sounds to me like I should choose between Jesus and beer. So what's the big deal? It's just a vacation for you."

" Oh, Daddy, it's not a vacation... but I know what you're saying. I know. In a letter C.S Lewis wrote to his friend Sheldon in A Severe Mercy, he talks about that very thing. Our emotions aren't made for that. I know that sooner or later we come back down to the ever-present stuff of life here. That's fine. But in the back of my mind and heart I'll always carry a bit of the North View with me, because it felt MORE real than..."

"More real than?"

"How people choose to live... I lose sight of God so many times, I can't hear His replies to my prayers. I can't feel His love all the time. But I know the only reality, the only real truth I've known is in Him. What I'm trying to say is He is more real than my feelings and answers my prayers whether I feel it or not. It's the same with his love for me."

"I'll go to church with you next Sunday I guess, but to the Sunny Baptist one. Not to..."

"I was just explaining what was on my heart. Not trying to get you to my church." Then she saw me again and greeted me. "Oh, hi Eldon."

"Hi," I said, having successfully removed the sugar dust from my face, but now had crumbs all over myself.

"I love you honey. I don't pretend to understand your enthusiasm for this stuff, but I do love you very very much. We both do, your mom and me," Mr. Solanski said.

"I love you too Daddy, with my whole heart. But Daddy, have you kept the Ten Commandments?"

"I guess so. I'm pretty good and all. I don't think about it."

Christine asked him, "You ever tell a lie?"

"Certainly. Everybody does."

"What does that make you?"

"Normal."

"If you killed someone, you're a murderer. So, what does telling a lie make you?"

"A liar I guess."

"You ever get angry at anyone, really angry, call them a fool?"

"A few times. What's this nonsense Christine?"

"Then by your own admission you're a liar and a murderer. Jesus said if anyone calls someone a fool he is guilty of murder, and in danger of hell."

"I thought you were going to tell me Jesus Christ would make me feel better, that He'll solve all my problems."

"Daddy, I won't lie to you. Becoming a Christian might cause you more problems than you had before. It only assures you of peace with God. You'll get persecution, temptations, trails and heartaches as well as eternal life with God."

"You're saying I'm not right with God yet?"

"If a building is on fire, would you complain about the wet blanket soiling your suit? Would you? Someday your whole life will be laid bare before God, every thought and every single thought examined. You'll face Him in judgment if you don't have Jesus Christ."

"He'll forgive me. God is good."

"You're trusting a good God to forgive you? How long would people call Judge Parker good if he released murderers and thieves? No. Only by having the righteousness of Christ can you be declared righteous."

"You're saying Christ took on my offenses against the judge? God! He took my penalty? So I don't have to be imprisoned?"

"Yes. You're drowning and don't know it."

"I never heard it put that way before honey," he replied. Then he said, "Sorry, but I got to go."

He just left us without looking back, me with my newspapers and leashes in the bag, her looking as concerned as could be.

"Hear any talk Eldon? Daddy did and he was worried."

"I get a laugh every time I go to Tinti's Christine. I listen to the old gents there yakking about football, crazy Rod, taxes, and then it's back to the taxes again. I haven't heard a single conversation about you. There or anywhere for that matter."

"We read the paper we got from May's Eldon."

"What do you think about joining me on a walk this morning? I only have two dogs to skate this time."

"Sounds fine to me."

As we walked the route, I was dropping papers off; picking up both Nappy, a poodle, and Tiny, a great Dane; I let her talk.

"Eldon, I know you're supposed to walk these dogs, but maybe I better hold the leash of that poodle, the Dane's pace is too much for her."

I agreed.

"So what have you heard Eldon?"

"I heard that the Greek fishermen are all holed up on account of the winds, there's a small craft advisory out. Only crazy Rod would fish today."

"He doesn't fish, he mows lawns silly boy."

"I know. Heyyyyy, you know what I like? I like the houses of the Greek fishermen Christine; they're not like the cookie-cutter houses of Hayford, nor like all the older weatherworn Victorian houses with their peeling paint we have. These simple cabins seem to fit our town best. Can't explain it. They're cool."

I was trying to get her mind off things. I hoped it was working.

"I know what you're trying to do... okay, let's see... I love the oak trees that line the Green, they are well over a hundred years old. I love their size, their strength and stability. Nature is beautiful. How's that?" She asked with a dramatic toss of her head, causing her hair to bounce a bit. I liked her auburn hair, which was gaining golden highlights from the sun. I already mentioned it was very thick and wavy.

"Go ahead Eldon... talk your magic talk." She smiled smile number five. Remember I told you she had five smiles whereas most folks have only one. This was smile five, her brightest.

"Another thing I like is in the winter on some of these magnificent trails the snows really work a spell out there that few people take time to notice. It glistens, the branches of those oaks shimmer and sparkle having been crystallized by old man winter. In the spring the same trails explode with life of all kinds, the brook which runs under the bridge of the band canopy starts to awaken."

"Speaking of the band canopy, I got some good news Eldon. The churches have put aside their differences for the date of the fundraiser. They'll all be involved."

"How did that happen I wonder."

"You'll never believe this."

"Hmm?"

"Helen Smhidt stopped fighting it. She called the churches and got them to work on the dates we had set up. SHE pushed the COMMITTEE into finally voting on allowing the use of the Green for the public!"

"I wonder why?"

" I don't know that, but she called my uncle and apologized for stuff. She was given a book by Babbs on the town, all those pictures of people here, I guess she read the letters at the end and changed her mind."

"One letter? Or letters?"

"Well, it's been updated. There were four pages of notes from some of the Black Panther men themselves whose lives were saved by my uncle George. But the book goes on to talk about the whole squadron. I guess she was afraid it'd be a book only on my uncle. Mr.

Smhidt's heroics were mentioned in the book, as well as Mr. Wallstein's."

"Really? Who got them to do those letters? Dig up that stuff?"

"Mr. Hophenetter wrote about the heroics of the men in his squadron. But the nicest note is from Mr. O'Brien."

"Why is that? You mean Bobby O'Brien?"

"There was no relation, and he wasn't from Apple Harbor but from Montgomery Alabama. His name was Joel O'Brien."

"So what did he say Christine?"

"Why the planes crashed that day. It had nothing to do with Uncle George. He didn't JUST write about their heroics but the bad stuff too."

I sighed and asked, "Why would that change Mrs. Smhidt's mind towards your uncle and the farm? She's been rather hostile for sometime towards the idea."

"It's a mystery to me, except her husband was in that battle too. Like I said, it mentions his heroics too, besides all their failings."

"Oh. I got to get me that book. But I don't want to know their failings really."

"It's not put real graphically. Mr. Hophenetter was kind. Eldon, oh, by the way! I have some smilegrams here. I want you to put them in your papers."

I didn't know what a smilegram was but I didn't want Christine to see the newspapers because of my drawings... and the articles on the Hendersons. When she grabbed a paper to insert her envelope marked "For Mr. Roman", another marked "For Mrs. Wallstien", and another " For Mrs. Smhidt"... I thought she might get upset at the drawing I did of Mrs. Wallstien. I tried to grab her hand before she could open the Town Section of the newspaper, but the Dane was giving me a lot of trouble.

"TINY!!!" I yelled.

Christine looked very disappointed at my drawings.

"Oh, Eldon, I don't think you better deliver these."

So I told her, "All right," in resignation, and we pulled them out. She placed the marked envelopes for them, and a few others, including the writer of the article who was on my route.

"Now I'll have to check each newspaper as we drop it off to be sure they get the right note, or coupon, or whatever a smilegram is."

"Oh poor baby!"

* * * * *

Now you're probably wondering what the effect of the news was on our school, and I wish I could report it had no affect whatsoever. But kids can be cruel, and some of the coldest comments came from the kids from her own church. They questioned her Christianity and her motives. She felt pretty awful about the whole thing, and having teachers ask her about her social security benefits didn't help matters much. People gawked and stared at her and would block her way. As she tried to make her way down the halls, they'd surround her and asked her rude questions. But instead of retreating back into her shell, she simply said, "I guess this shows I need forgiveness too, huh?" When Balligrino yelled, "You hypocrite! Phony!" she would answer back, "You're right. Pray for me. You have no idea how very weak I am and how much I need Jesus."

That wasn't the answer they expected. She wasn't defending herself or making excuses. She didn't once try to justify herself. Eventually this took the wind out of their sails and by Friday, kids left her alone. She had several fans that thought it was totally cool, her fooling everyone. But that didn't encourage her. A couple of girls from her church met her in the library, they chatted with her and I saw her laughing and shaking her head yes. They were talking girl talk, but that seemed to do her more good than a thousand greeting cards could.

So by Friday the only one who cared was Mrs. Kei. She wanted Christine to play the part of an old woman in a school play late this summer. Not exactly what she wanted to do. Christine said she hadn't even tried out for the part yet, but Mrs. Kei told her it was hers if she wanted it. So Christine had to decide between a part in a play or North View Christian summer camp.

When I opened my schoolbook bag, I found a smilegram for myself.

"Eldon, Thank you for being my friend, Christine."

Her PS really undid me.

"I'm glad that you have eyes to absorb the wonders around you, not that life is all wonderful, but even in the midst of our pains… we have Christ, and HE can transform our vision from gloomy (which is a lie), to truth. We are then strong enough to not escape things, nor be naive about people's natures… I making sense?? I am very proud of you my friend. You're great!! I just found out today I've been accepted at the Academy, so this will be my last year in Apple Harbor. Your pal, Christine."

That unplugged my heating pad. Academy?

It was like the world suddenly choked all the life out of everything, the skies turned gray and all I saw was darkness, shadows, and misery creeping about me. I didn't notice anything the rest of that day. My best friend was leaving. The only thing I do remember from that day is I went to Crachet's Barbershop and asked for a shave.

"What do you want a shave for boy? The cat could lick off those whiskers if you put a little milk on it," Mr. Crachet said, laughing. The card players laughed too, Russ Peters and Bobby O'Brien.

"Please, my friend Christine is right behind me, she was talking to Kasie and…"

Mr. Crachet gave his friends a knowing look, and applied the shaving cream to my face. It was very hot because he had a special container to preheat it, and he sharpened the blade on a razor strop. Christine walked in as he was sharpening the blade. I could feel every swipe of the blade across my face.

Christine sat down. She was wearing a pleated skirt with laces.

" Boy is this a thick beard, I don't think I've had a beard so thick in a man so young before. Wasn't I just saying that Russ and Bobby?"

" Yeah, yeah, I don't think I've ever heard of such a thing," Russ said.

Mrs. Wallstien's Smilegram

She was reading her Bible. I don't think she was buying any of this.

"So, where's that shadow of yours young lady?" Mr. Crachet asked Christine.

"Kasie went to get a box with James from Mrs. Hophenetter, pretty cool, huh Eldon?"

The blade was right over my upper lip. I couldn't answer her.

She smiled smile number two and went on reading her Bible as Mr. Crachet washed off the remaining shaving cream, and applied some of the best smelling cologne to my face.

"The ladies love this stuff," he whispered.

Then he cut my hair, but not too much. He knew how I liked my hair. In those days a little length was a good thing. He put a bit of that hair tonic in it, I was going to say to him "Don't," but as he already had the stuff in there.

Christine looked at the finished product, me with my hair actually combed and she said, "Wow! I wouldn't recognize you"

I tipped Mr. Crachet.

As we left the shop and were walking on our way to who knows where, Christine asked me about weird dreams, so I told her a dozy.

"My dream involved me coming into far too much money, and being truly upset about it. So I have some relatives come over who help me decide how to spend it."

"You were upset about having too much money Eldon?"

"Yes, some people I didn't know I was related to. Mom and Dad had moved out, Kasie too, because somehow the idea of me coming into all the money offended them terribly."

"Offended them? Really?" Christine asked, laughing at me.

"Yeah. They were sooo offended! So these unknown relatives came over, these relatives were very strange people, they seemed to me to be dumber than rocks. They drove loud obnoxious cars, and these cars were thrown together after an explosion at Smhidt's construction. They drank the most foul smelling rum and hunted moosealopes in the woods at night. You told me I needed to honor these relatives so I went hunting with them. Oh, it was sad, terribly sad. One of the boys was so dumb he shot at his own shadow in the tent, thinking it was a moosealope. It got below freezing, and the rest of our hunting trip was pure misery, as these clowns never even saw a moosealope, and didn't realize the bullets they had brought were little better than punching holes in tents or my windshield. Which they did."

"What's a moosealope?" Christine asked me between her giggles.

"It's the result of a marriage between a moose and an antelope. So instead of investing in their schemes, I poured my money into the research of genetically altered foods done at the local university by a very young student, a twelve-year-old genius. He discovered a way to introduce the DNA and genes of the Beluga whale into smoked salmon, which somehow replicated itself and created a sandwich... a heavenly sandwich the size of the whale with a taste out of this world, to die for. So I opened a grocery store selling Genetically Altered Foods."

"I think I'll stay away from your store Mr. Eldon Cooper," she said, grabbing me on the shoulder.

"Whatever for Christine? You drove me to that madness you know."

"In WHAT way?" She feigned grave offense.

"By telling me to be honorable to unknown relatives."

"Like you'd ever listen to me?" she said, putting on a haughty demeanor.

My motor mouth, at least motoring around her, made me feel alive. And she laughed, so it wasn't too awful.

We sat down at Tinti's. Babbs asked us what we wanted, I ordered a double cheeseburger, fries and cherry malt, and Christine ordered a salad about the size of a tea bag. I asked for two straws but Christine wasn't very thirsty.

Then she told me about her dream.

"I had a dream too. I saw a beautiful crystal river that glistens, I swam in it and it gave my skin an amber glow, the glow of health. My grandfather, also a believer joined me. He looks to be about twenty or so. He is rejoicing in Christ, praising Him and celebrating this incredible freedom."

"And," she went on, "the very air is saturated with peace. A peace you never knew. No sense of hurry here.

"The very grass held my attention, sprinkled about with an array of multi-colored flowers and flowing, as it were, to a music I can feel. The pines and oaks line the sides of these paths; I wonder where it leads. No brown leafs anywhere.

"Suddenly I come across a vast field and see dinosaurs, brontosaurs and the T-Rex, cavorting with hundreds of children. Among them are lions, sheep, cattle, panthers and monkeys. It looks like an overgrown zoo, only each animal, though tame, is certainly not placid. They're in complete joy, abandoning themselves over to their Maker.

"I could not believe the light there, reflecting off everything without shadows. I seemed to understand what Christ's death and resurrection meant even better. I knew people without knowing their names. I heard singing there, angels, everything, it was just sooo perfect!"

I wasn't sure what to say to that. But it made her happy and I guessed that was the important thing. I looked over to our left from the booth we were seated at, I saw Mrs. Wallstien looking her burger over as if she wasn't sure if she should eat it or shoot it. Her eyes were big and they were only getting bigger. Then it finally dawned on me that it wasn't the burger she was looking at so much, but some note. I saw the envelope on the table in front of her; it had a bright yellow smile on it. I recognized the flowery drawing style as Christine's. She was reading the smilegram and looking like she was going to get sick. I was hoping she wouldn't do that. I was hungry after all and certainly didn't think that would help my consumption. Then, unfortunately her eye caught mine, and she spotted Christine sitting right across from me. Then she ran away from her booth as if someone was trying to steal one of her blessed cows. I noticed she had left her burger there too.

But before I could think about it much longer, my own burger was there, along with my malt and fries.

Christine was thirsty after all, so she had a few sips, a few sips, which turned into a few more. I was about to take a bite of my double cheeseburger when Christine asked me if perhaps I'd mind sharing half of it. So I cut it in half. It was the least I could do.

About that time I overheard Doctor Anderson ask Mr. Rowe if perhaps they had already noticed their corn growing. He complained that the ground was too wet and the seed was terribly inferior, that he had bought the seed from that same clown who fattens up his cows on molasses before he sells them.

"Yeah, the beef from there taste like molasses no matter what you do."

"So why did you buy it from him then?" I heard Dr. Anderson ask him.

"I liked the price I guess."

My attention perked up, as well as Christine's, when we overheard Mr. Rowe mention something about a bunch of them from the Lutheran Church going over to visit the Hendersons. They brought over some groceries in his 1952 Chevy Deluxe that was a hunter green car. I imagined that he'd dump a lot of that sweet beef on the Hendersons. He was kind of a cheap guy, used comic strips for wallpaper and yet had more money than he needed really.

"Irene got together all sorts of food for them," Mr. Rowe said in that voice which always sounded like he had jogged a dozen blocks. "Quality beef and pork ribs and all kinds of canned vegetables. Those jars and wax sure come in handy. Glad Irene knows canning."

"You didn't give them the molasses beef I hope?" Dr. Anderson asked, sounding upset.

"I wouldn't think of that. Not for George. Mary gave her some prized tomato plants, you know, Mary Nelson? One of the coaches from the basketball team brought over a ton of coupons and a turkey. Over half of the coupons are ten years expired though."

Christine found this particularly funny, and couldn't stop laughing. At that moment I saw that Mrs. Wallstien was talking to Babbs, pointing to us, and handing her a five-dollar bill. Babbs smiled and put a bill and the five in her apron pocket. Neither of them seemed to notice that I saw them.

"Christine, I'm curious, what did you write to Mrs. Wallstien in that note?"

"I asked her if she had anything in her life that might turn on her."

"Excuse me?"

"I told her I knew about her losing her brothers in the Second World War, and that I was terribly sorry. But I thought she should forgive God, and move on, otherwise the bitterness will turn on her. It'll be all she has left."

"Forgive God? That's odd."

"Is it really Eldon? It's not because He's done anything wrong and is in need of our forgiveness, no. I explained that too. But sometimes, He allows a horrible thing to happen, for whatever reasons. We have to forgive God, or life, ourselves, whoever."

I was trying to turn the conversation around a bit to something romantic, but she had known me my whole life and would figure it was some kind of joke, something new and funny. Nothing would come out. I simply asked her.

"How did you learn this stuff, think this way?"

"Silence is a great teacher, pain is too. When Mom was in the hospital for her emotional problems, she used to talk about death incessantly. I didn't want to be around her. She was drowning and no one seemed to be able to help. Doctors, even some faith healers came by her room and shouted at the devil to come out. They blamed her for not having faith to be healed. But it's not about that."

"What do you mean?"

"Mom's mind and heart was already in the Lord's hands, as well as Mrs. Wallstien's brothers. I can't judge life by my ideas of how it should be. I believe with all of me that God used Mom… even there… for His pleasure, His glory."

"I hated the smells of that hospital Christine, but we came by."

"The white halls, disinfectant, and some of the staff were mean, I know. I appreciated everything you and Kasie did for my mom. Just seeing her."

"You really believe God can use… broken people?"

" Yes, I learned to watch and listen a lot I guess. I learned how very little I needed to be happy. I saw how He can really be trusted Eldon; it's not just easy nice words for me."

"You sure seem to have something there."

"I have Him, yeah."

"She lost her brothers Christine?"

"Yep. Two days just before Mr. Henderson rescued the Blank Panthers, they died with that squadron. They weren't originally part of that squadron but many of the squads had lost so many men following D-Day that they regrouped into other formations. It's weird but they never knew those guys from Apple Harbor, although their sister lived there for years by then. They just never visited her here in Connecticut."

"I guess this thing with the fundraiser was like opening her sores then. Especially since she knew what Mr. Henderson did just two days after her brothers died."

"Yeah. She used to be a prayer warrior. Your grandmother showed me some pictures of them together during the war, leading Prayer meetings. Her prayers stopped with the telegraph from the war department."

"She's been mad all those years?"

"There is a verse in the Bible that says, 'Train up a child in the way he should go, and when he is old he will not depart from it. I believe she'll come around. Maybe not tomorrow but someday'."

Then she smiled that smile which showed so many of her teeth. That was my favorite smile. It looked like she was ready to laugh, or burst forth like a flower, into joy.

How was I going to go on with her leaving? I went up to pay the bill for our food, but Babbs said, "Someone said to say 'Thank you Christine, Bless your heart for that kind note.' She paid the bill, for you too Eldon."

"But I was going to pay for us both."

"What do you think this is, a date?!" Christine exclaimed sounding exasperated. I thought she was mad but then saw by her face she was teasing me. Maybe I was wearing my heart on my sleeve after all? Probably she wasn't aware of how I felt. But did it matter? She was leaving soon. Why couldn't I say anything? How could we be joking about a dream one minute then talking about faith through the storms the next? She had me on a roller coaster ride I did not understand, but looking across at her as we walked, side by side... I really didn't mind at all.

— chapter 15 —

Henderson's Day?

It was late that night Mr. Henderson couldn't sleep.

He got up, looked over at his wife and brushed the hair from her face. "I could've done you better," he said, sitting besides her.

He was thinking about the debts, wondering why his sons never took over the farm, wondering why seed and equipment seemed so unnecessarily expensive, whereas the prices the elevator gave him hardly seemed worth it. He went downstairs in his pajamas. He lit a Coleman gas lamp, the one his brother had bought him. It was a hint to take a vacation, a camping trip. Just like the magazines his brother had subscribed to for him, those magazines which told about all the exotic places they never could afford. His brother could. He loved his brother but was happy to see their family leave whenever they came around on the holidays.

He noticed his grandfather clock was five minutes off. He set it right by the pocket watch his grandfather had given him, a picture of old Number 7 was on the front, our local legend. It was a very reliable watch. He became aware that the other clocks were off, just a minute on the mantel clock, but ten on the hall one.

He ground up some coffee beans, placed them in the percolator, primed the pump and prepared a bucket under it. He put some wood in his stove, lit a fire, and put a few tea bags in the teapot over the fire. He forgot all about the coffee and instead after about fifteen minutes had Earl Grey tea instead.

It was then, having sat down at the table that he looked at Bear, his German shepherd-chow mix and sighed.

"Oh, what difference does it make anyways. I never wanted to take someone's charity. I wanted to..."

His voice trailed off.

The tea was remarkably good. He was aware the tea had a hint of coffee taste to it. Then he saw that he had grabbed the percolator, which he had forgotten he had put water in, and had set on the stove right besides the teapot.

"I need some fresh air. Come on Bear."

He looked around at his barn, his newest barn that Jason Smhidt had been so kind as to volunteer to build him. It must have been the finest construction he'd ever seen. He remembered the old barn. Then it all started to come back to him. One memory at a time, they marched back to revive him.

He saw his niece Christine at six years old swinging on that old tire, laughing. He saw James and me having a water balloon fight from the loft, bombing everyone. He saw Kasie try to stand on Jake, the quarter horse. She fell on her butt because she had heals on, and he had no saddle so Jake reared up on her.

Then he remembered some of the things Christine had said so much, about the Lord's goodness and mercy.

"I love those kids Lord, I really do."

He spoke to the heavens, seeing for the first time how very pretty it was out here. The clouds were eclipsing the moon in silver-gray streaks as honking geese flew overhead. A soft breeze stirred in the apple blossoms, the pines, it sounded like whispers, and the clouds looked more and more like angel wings.

He suddenly realized how much he loved this life of his fathers.

"I understand Lord. Thank you."

A set of headlights flickered on and off, and then faded until they went out completely by the end of his property. Mr. Henderson supposed that some young person had driven into the apple trees in spite of the white paint. Perhaps they were drunk. He looked to Bear, who appeared just as eager to investigate. So he got into his old 1928 Ford Phaeton and drove it down there, with Bear besides him. He saw a van, with bright bold letters on the side, inside the sky of a mural of an eagle gliding over a valley. The hood of the van was up. A young black man was working under it, oblivious to Mr. Henderson.

A young woman, also black was sitting in the front, resting. He noticed band equipment, and a white couple resting in the back, reading the Bible together.

" You need some help?"

" My alternator's shot, keeps killing the battery. Can't get any parts till the morning. I guess we're in trouble. Maybe you can give us a ride to a motel? I'm Clarence by the way."

"George. My name is George Henderson."

Mr. Henderson looked closely at the van and noticed the small cross on the side of the canyon, and the Bible verse underneath. They didn't seem dangerous. The men's hair wasn't too long and they didn't have a crazed look in their eyes. They didn't appear like they had much money either.

"Why don't you stay at my farm tonight?"

The man in the front, whose name was Clarence said, "No, that won't be necessary."

But his wife said, "Yes. I just want to take a three-hour bath, and read a book and be left alone."

So that about settled it. He drove them to the front door, and led them to the kitchen, then woke up Mrs. Henderson. She really didn't want to be woken up, she complained and turned over, but he was persistent, and finally she got up to visit her guests.

Now Mr. Henderson didn't know the "WHAT-NOTS " band from any other country gospel band. But in our small town of Apple Harbor they were pretty big, and appreciated, even though they came from Johnson City Tennessee. So far away, yet Mrs. Rowe, Babbs, the Nelsons, Fred and Jenkins all talked about that band they saw in evil New Haven. They had never glowed so as when they talked about that band at Tinti's, well, except for Babbs. Even Jenkins smiled. But Mr. Henderson had no clue who these people were, and they seemed to be nice people who were in trouble.

That next morning James and I showed up at their door. We had just gotten word that the band, the "Wannabes", a polka band that my mom liked a lot would not be at the fundraiser today. Their lead singer got sick off some bad hot dish at a potluck at our own Baptist church.

We had seen him get sick right at the front of the basement pulpit, and it wasn't a pretty sight. He was singing, performing with his band, as we ate. Then suddenly he stopped, ran... and, well, you know the rest.

So we told Mrs. Henderson about that, and James recognized their guests but didn't say anything, except to me. After all, he listened to everything from heavy metal to classical music, and everything else around the bend too. He just loved music.

Clarence spoke up from the kitchen table. "You mind if we play at your town's event? Could you arrange that?"

"Not like we're going anywhere," the man to his right spoke, obviously a bass. A deep deep bass.

"What kind of rock you play?" Mrs. Henderson asked him.

"Rock, country, jazz... but with a Christian sound," the black lady said soothing Mrs. Henderson. She must've known how to push the right buttons because now Mrs. Henderson was smiling wide and big.

So the fundraiser had music then, and once word got out that the "What-Nots" were there, people flooded the parking lot of city hall and downtown Apple Harbor.

With the sound system they had, it didn't take much to get people to gather. You could hear it for miles. Martha Wallstien, Mabel's sister thought we should charge for seats at the show, but that wasn't too bright. People brought their own lawn chairs to the Green after all, besides the park benches. So we had everything roped around the Green by the police's brand new yellow tape. That was the best we could do. But with so many people selling crafts and jewelry, so many tables set around the parameters of the Green, nobody could sneak in anyways. Mrs. Smhidt took to selling the tickets at the only entrance. She charged about two dollars for kids and two fifty for adults. We didn't get to many complaints. That included a free drink of your choice at the concession stand.

Old Salt and Duane Franks... Smokey, ran the concession stand. The banner above the sky blue concession stand read: 'The Salty Frank. Why not?' The smell coming from that stand was enough to draw a crowd all day. They grilled burgers, franks and on a separate grill; Old Salt did fish. I never saw them in better form. They were yelling "Order up!" and the church ladies were racing the orders to everyone quicker than I ever saw, even at Tinti's. The only glitch in the day there was when Balligrino and that Doglas kid both decided to contribute their own brownies to the tray of brownies. Theirs had garlic and hot pepper pieces. They could only sneak in a few. Just as they were about to sneak out of the kitchen area of the concession stand, Babbs walked in on them.

"Oh you two dears," she cried out. "You've come to help us out!"

So she handed them aprons and they were taking orders from everyone, including James, Christine, Kasie and me. Now Babbs had noticed how they had eye-balled four particular brownies, so she set them aside for the free dinners for them, and two of their friends after everyone else was served. She didn't mean any harm you know.

The potato sack race was supposed to be for kids only, ages four to eighteen. But somehow Mr. Jenkins got involved; he was having the time of his life. It was good to see that.

He didn't win, but go tell that to his face. He was all smiles that day. Christine came in second to Kasie, my sister, who hopped like a pro. Actually Mr. Jenkins lost dead last to his grandson and granddaughter, twins, both four. But by the look on his face you'd have thought he'd won.

The sun was beautiful that day, it looked as if it had waited all spring to store up some of that warmth, that loveliness all over. It seemed to have worked its magic on just about all of us, or perhaps it was the weeks of prayers that Christine, and Babbs and sometimes we offered up for the day. It wasn't too hot, there was a mild breeze from the south, which caught the scents of lavender flowers, and raised bushes just coming on their own. Everywhere you went on the Green, whether the band canopy area to hear the "What-Nots", or the tiny bridge over the brook with its cherry blossoms, you'd have caught a whiff of those lovely flowers. I noticed the food scents all day too, I must've spent several weeks' allowance on burgers, cotton candy, hot dogs, pizza and malts. But I was buying for two of us you see. I don't mean my sister.

Just as the "What-Nots" broke up for a break, Frank approached Clarence of that group and asked him some questions about the songs they had sung. They were wonderful songs, and he had been thinking lately about Christine's faith in Christ. Just as he was asking these questions, Christine and I walked by them, carrying a large pink cotton candy.

"Christine?" her father asked her. "I was just about to ask Clarence here how I can know your Jesus. Why don't you tell me?"

"You need to know you didn't keep the Ten Commandments, that you're not right with God's absolute perfection."

"I have no problem understanding that honey."

"So you understand you need to be forgiven, right?"

"Yeah, I do."

"You're not teasing?"

"I wouldn't tease about this, no," Frank said.

"Pray with me this prayer then, but only if you agree with it… I'll stop after a while each time so you can think about it, okay…

"Lord Jesus, I ask you to come into my life, because when you died on that cross I died with you. My sins died with you, every mistake I ever made, every failure, you washed me clean.

"You, God in the flesh, walking as a man, you died… for… me.

"You wanted to make things right between us…

"When You rose from the dead, when your Father brought you back to life, He was saying 'This sacrifice is acceptable.' Thank you Lord for giving me eternal life, like it says in John 3;16, 'For God did so loved the world, He sent His only begotten son, that whosoever… that's you… believes in Him shall not perish but have everlasting life!'

"We pray this in Jesus' name, Amen."

She said 'Amen', now *that* felt like a proper prayer! He had agreed and repeated everything in that prayer, so he prayed it. Clarence and his wife had come along while we were praying, Christine luring him in, me praying he wouldn't get away. Clarence and his wife were the second people to welcome him into God's family. Christine was the first.

" Ohhhhh, Daddddy!!" she cried out, hugging him, crying and laughing, laughing and crying.

The "What-Nots" were just getting off their break, so we walked them back to the canopy. They performed *Amazing Grace* in honor of "A new, unnamed brother among us," and a few other gospel songs, and hymns. *It Is Well With My Soul*, *As a Deer Panteth For The Waters*, and several others. I was sitting with James and Kasie, to give Christine some private time with her father and mother. I saw Mrs. Wallstein in the very back, at the last row of seats. She wouldn't stand, I guess she didn't want to draw attention to herself; most of us were standing, clapping as we sang some of the faster gospel music. But she wasn't leaving either. I also saw Craig there, with his father. He looked like a happier kid than I had seen in a long time. Yes, they played Christian rock.

The funny thing is, that's when Helen Smhidt came to the front. She wasn't a fan of the music, but was looking for Christine. But she enjoyed the music in spite of herself, and I saw her laughing at herself as she would dance to the beat. She couldn't dance to save her life, but these dances weren't too difficult if you know what I mean. You just swayed, then everyone swayed with you, and the sway would move from right to left of the whole audience. You probably think that started in some football game, but it didn't. It got its patent at some Apple Harbor church wayyy wayyy back in the twenties. But don't worry. We won't sue you for using it now and then. Just remember where it came from.

With the sale of the books that Mrs. Hophenetter had printed up, and the sale of everything else as well… food, music, events, the Hendersons made more than enough to pay off their debts and then some. No one at all expected or even hoped for that. I think there's a verse about that too… "To Him who is far better able to do far more exceedingly more than we can imagine…" something like that. Christine would know. They added some rooms to the farmhouse with the kind help of Smhidt Construction, not because Jason thought Judge Parker had anything on him anymore, but because he had read that book Mrs. Hophenetter made. He had seen how George Henderson had saved his father's life.

They built additions to their farmhouse you see, to make a Bed and

Breakfast. It was a good investment. People came from as far away as New York City to show their kids a real farm, real sheep and goats and to ride Jake, and maybe even fly in a biplane, or tour Apple Harbor in that 1928 Ford.

Old Salt hired Smoky Franks full time to take care of cooking while he was at sea, and for the rest of the year for that matter. The college boy he had was leaving soon anyhow, having graduated, and Old Salt would start fishing the Atlantic next week.

The last few minutes of the Fund-raiser we saw Bobby Doglas, Balligrino and two of their friends make a mad dash for the water fountain. They had eaten their own brownies.

I walked Christine home, carrying a bare umbrella. You have a sister like Kasie and you'll do unusual things too. Christine was giving me the same look you are.

"Why are you carrying a skeleton of an umbrella Eldon?" she asked me.

"It's going to rain, see." I pointed to a large gray cloud, coming in from the south. It would be a warm rain. We could see the cloud that looked like watercolor paint streaked, so I knew that it already was raining out there.

"But it's only the metal frame Eldon, what good..."

"We need to be selective about the drops we allow to enter our domain, after all, not just any old drop should have the thrill of getting us, right?"

"Uhhhh, okay, but what's going on with that bottle of shampoo in your pocket?"

"Oh, one must always be prepared, right?"

She was laughing again at my quirky sense of humor. When you have a sister like Kasie you develop a quirky sense of humor.

"I just realized something Eldon, this umbrella is a receiver. It picks up the refrains of sun drop's music, those unnamed symphonies that only friends like you... and other sane people can hear."

"Yes Christine! Don't pity those poor fools..." I said as people passed us by, past Mays Hobby store, past the cobblestones now wet. "I pity them, for they can't hear our music!"

"I certainly do," she said, sounding like Hardy in Laurel and Hardy.

We got odd looks, but when it rained I bet they felt foolish not having an umbrella like we did. It wouldn't be until later that summer that I'd realize how much she meant to me, but that comes later.

Her life at the academy away from Apple Harbor, what happens to the rest of us here, it will be told, yes, don't worry about it.

You know, I was wondering, has anyone ever told you that you make an awful lot of faces when you read?

the end... but not quite.